A SLOANE MONR

# BLACK DIAMOND DEATH

## CHERYL BRADSHAW
*NEW YORK TIMES* BESTSELLING AUTHOR

This book is a work of fiction. Names, characters, places, businesses, and incidents either are the products of the author's imagination or are used in a fictitious manner. Any similarity to events or locales or persons, living or dead, is entirely coincidental.

First Edition June 2011
Second Edition August 2019
Copyright © 2011 by Cheryl Bradshaw
Revised © 2019 by Cheryl Bradshaw
Cover Design Copyright 2019 © Indie Designz
All rights reserved.

No part of this publication may be reproduced, stored or transmitted, given away or re-sold in any form, or by any means whatsoever (electronic, mechanical, etc.) without the prior written permission and consent of the author. Thank you for being respectful of the hard work of the author.

*To Kylie for the miracle that you are in my life
And to Grandpa Butch—I miss you*

You can fool all the people some of the time,
and some of the people all the time,
but you cannot fool all the people all the time.

—Abraham Lincoln

# CHAPTER 1

The air was calm, but Charlotte Halliwell was restless. She had a decision to make so she did what she always did when push came to shove—she shoved back. Skiing had always been her release, her go-to when the anxieties and demons of life became too difficult to bear. There was something about being surrounded by fresh powder and clean air that reminded her of what it felt like to be alive again. She could stand on a mountaintop with a world of trouble on her mind, but it didn't matter. Every care dissolved just like the snow soon would, leaving tiny patches of white, mere remnants of a ski slope that once provided the town's entertainment for the season.

Today was important.

Today was the day Charlotte would have lunch with Audrey, her sister, and reveal a grave secret she'd kept to herself ... until today.

Rounding the last narrow pass on the ski slope, Charlotte traveled downhill through the trees. But something was wrong. Something didn't *feel* right.

Her tongue had gone numb. When her teeth brushed against it, she felt nothing, like it wasn't even there, and her throat was inflamed with an intense burning, like a strand of lit matches was pressed hard against it.

Charlotte wondered if she was getting sick. The flu *had* been making its way around town. But if it *was* the flu, why had she lost all feeling in her face? And why were her eyes so blurry?

She ran a gloved hand across her goggles, but it didn't help. She squeezed her eyes shut and opened them again, but the trail in front of her was still too hazy to make out. With what little force she had left, she jammed her poles into the snow, trying to stop, but the slope was too steep, and her fingers had turned to frail shards of ice.

*What is happening to me?*

In a panic, she gasped for air, but there wasn't any.

She tried to cry out, but she was alone, and in her hysteria she realized she'd felt a similar feeling once before, and she knew what it meant.

She was dying.

# CHAPTER 2

*Fifteen minutes later*

The car skidded across the road making an *rrrt* sound, the kind of sound that propelled people from their chairs and to the window to catch a glimpse of the potential train wreck outside. Only I was on a lonely stretch of road with nothing but the pine trees spinning around me. In desperation I struggled to remember the words my grandfather once taught me: *Don't slam on the brake pedal, Sloane. Tap it. Don't turn the wheel in the direction of the skid, rotate away from it.* Or had he said to turn *into* the skid, and why couldn't I remember?

The wheels gripped the road in an attempt to regain traction. I tapped the brake and fought off the urge to slam both heels into the pedal simultaneously. The car lurched from side to side before it steadied and I regained control again.

I sat there for a moment, allowing the car to idle while I breathed. Then I put it back into gear, driving at a snail's pace until the iron gates of the ski resort came into view.

A boy wearing padded black trousers, a black and white ski jacket, and gloves waved me over.

"Hello ma'am," he said. "Welcome to Wildwood. Valet?"

I nodded.

He pointed toward the resort. "Drive around this corner to the roundabout and give your keys to Phil at the front. He'll take good care of you."

Wildwood, Park City's newest ski resort, attracted a diverse group of guests from locals to celebrities. I handed the keys of my car to the valet and entered the resort, stopping to look at the historical photographs lining the walls of the interior. Some depicted the Daily Mining Company circa 1980, while others showed off historic Main Street predating the fire that had almost left it a ghost town.

Groups of skiers hustled back and forth through the hallway, eager to reach the lift and soar to their destinations. I thawed my fingers in front of the fire and walked to the front desk. A girl wearing a fitted red suit-coat accented with a bronze name tag greeted me. She had bright rosy cheeks and bleach-blond hair pulled back into a tight bun, reminding me of a female version of a nutcracker.

"Hi there," she said. "Welcome to Wildwood Resort. What can I do for you today?"

"I'm here to see Marty Langston," I said.

"Do you have an appointment?"

I nodded.

She smiled. "Great. What's the name?"

"Sloane."

"And the last name?"

"Monroe."

She picked up the phone receiver, pressed a button, and waited. "Mr. Langston? There's a woman at the front desk to see you by the name of Sloane Monroe. What's that? Oh, sure. I'll tell her."

She placed the phone back on the receiver and glanced past me, winking at a male employee walking by. He smiled back, and she seemed to forget all about me.

"Can you point me in the direction of Marty's office?" I asked.

"Oh, umm, he'll be right with you," she said.

Marty emerged from a corner office a minute later, wearing a smart gray suit and a necktie that had partially come undone.

He extended his arms and pulled me close. "It's good to see you, Sloane."

We broke from the embrace, and I reached for his tie and straightened it. "How's the new CEO?"

"On about two hours of sleep a night and all the coffee I can stand." He ran a hand through his hair and shook his head. "My hair's becoming more salt than pepper every day."

"It looks great on you," I said.

He spread his arms. "What do you think? Have you had the chance to check the place out yet?"

I shook my head.

"What about lunch?" he said. "Are you hungry?"

"A cup of tea would be nice."

"Let's grab a couple drinks, and I'll show you around."

The resort café included three sections: a quaint bar area, a much larger open dining section with tables and chairs in various sizes, and a more intimate section with arched windows that offered a panoramic view of a few of the ski slopes. I stopped for a moment and watched a skier schuss her way downhill.

Marty pointed to a selection of teas on the countertop. "Black tea if memory serves?"

I nodded.

He glanced out the window. "Spectacular view, isn't it?"

"Fantastic," I said. "The resort is stunning."

"So how about it?"

"How about what?"

He pointed to a group of people who appeared to be on skis for the first time. "Say the word, and I'll make it happen. It's never too late to learn."

I laughed. "I'm much more of a beach bunny than a snow bunny, Marty."

He shrugged. "It's never too late to change."

The bunny slope wasn't my idea of a good time. It made no sense to me why anyone would subject themselves to zero-degree temperatures when they could appreciate the mounds of white from inside, nestled by the glow of a stoked fire. Cold was my kryptonite, and yet I endured it because I enjoyed life in this city.

The café was deserted except for one other person, a woman seated in the open dining section. She had long, ash-blond hair and wore a bright red shirt that was tight enough to bounce a quarter off of it.

Marty handed me a cup of tea, grabbed himself a coffee, and we sat down.

"You're still my favorite client, you know," I said.

"Because of my rugged good looks?"

I laughed.

Marty had been adopted at birth. Years earlier when he became mayor of Park City, he experienced a sudden urge to find Kate, his birth mother. It took me three months to find her, but eventually my hard work paid off.

"How goes the private investigator business these days?" he asked.

"I haven't found a case I can sink my teeth into at the moment. But I can't complain."

"No one threaten your life this week, eh? Sounds boring."

"The week's not over yet," I said.

"Can't convince you to go back to basics even if I wanted you to, right?"

"And risk the thrill of the chase? Never."

The woman in the red shirt glanced at her watch and rapped her manicured nails on the table. She looked nervous and like she'd grown tired of sitting there, waiting. A waiter approached her and offered to refresh her drink. She handed him her empty glass, and he brought her a new one.

Marty took a few swigs of coffee and rose from his chair. "Ready for the grand tour?"

I wasn't. We'd only just put our drinks down, but over the years, I'd learned Marty was fidgety. He never sat for long.

I stood, intertwined my arm in his, and we walked out of the café. We didn't make it far before footsteps approached from behind. We turned.

"Excuse me," the man said. "I'm sorry to interrupt. Mr. Langston, there's an urgent phone call for you."

"I'm sure it can wait," Marty said. "Take a message. I'm on break for the rest of the afternoon."

"It's just … you should take the call, sir."

"Why?" Marty asked. "What's the urgency?"

The man glanced at me and then at Marty. "I'd rather not say. Can we talk in your office?"

"You can speak in front of Miss Monroe," Marty said. "She's like family to me."

The man grimaced and then said, "We just got a call from Ski Patrol. Something's happened on one of the ski runs. It sounds serious."

Marty shifted his gaze from the man to me and sighed. "I'm sorry. I better see what's going on. Can you wait here for a minute?"

I nodded, and Marty followed the man down the hall.

With nothing to stimulate me, I turned my attention to the woman in the red shirt. She glanced down at her watch, sighing in frustration before slinging her handbag over her shoulder and walking out of the room.

Marty returned a few minutes later with a stern look on his face. "Forgive me, my dear. Duty calls. Rain check on the tour?"

I nodded. "Sure. Is everything all right?"

He shook his head. "I'm afraid not. There's been a horrible accident."

# CHAPTER 3

Marty left without offering additional details about what had happened. I lingered around for a few minutes, wanting to know more, and then decided despite my curiosity, it was best for me to leave. I pushed the resort door open and was met with a forceful tug on the other side. It launched me forward, bringing me up close and personal with a familiar face I hadn't seen in a while.

"Well, well, if it isn't Little Miss Nosy," he said. "Let me guess, you just *happened* to be in the neighborhood, right?"

"Give it a rest, Coop." I said. "I was here to see Marty."

Detective Drake Cooper stood six foot five and used every inch of his stalwartly physique to browbeat anyone who stood in his way. He had an oval-shaped head and a jacked-up nose that sloped at a severe angle. For a senior citizen, his body was that of a man half his age.

"Look," I said, "I know about the accident."

I figured I was already there, so why not do some fishing?

"And you came by this information how?" he asked.

"Marty told me."

Coop swung the door all the way open. "Why don't you run along and let the big boys do their job?"

Unfortunately for me, the fish weren't biting today.

Coop stepped in front of me, blocking the lobby entrance like a concrete barrier. "Anytime, schweetheart."

Coop had an old-school mindset. In his eyes, I didn't deserve the role of private investigator. I stood in the way of *real* police work. Except I *had* earned the right, and on a few occasions I'd proved myself, which had made him resent me all the more. Three years earlier, he'd lost his dream of becoming Park City's next chief of police to Wade Sheppard, a detective with half the experience. Life had dealt him an unfair hand, and ever since, everyone else had paid the price.

I wrapped my coat around me and headed outside. There were days Coop pushed, and I pushed back. But I'd seen darkness in his eyes today, a grim look that made me hold back. Whatever he was doing at the resort, I feared I'd find out soon enough.

# CHAPTER 4

Lord Berkeley, a.k.a. Boo, my spunky West Highland Terrier, spun around in circles when I walked through the door. I scooped him up and carried him to the kitchen.

"And how's your day going, Boo, hmmm?" I said. "Miss me?"

He tilted his head to the side and wagged his tail.

"I'll take that as a yes."

I fished through the dishwasher for my favorite mug. It was white and had a saying written across the front: *Man cannot live on chocolate alone, but a woman sure can.* I made some tea and thought about the look on Marty's face right before we'd parted. It worried me. I grabbed my phone and dialed his number. He didn't answer.

A few minutes later, my phone rang. I looked at the screen, thinking it would be Marty, but a different man in my life was calling.

"Hey, Nick," I said.

Nick was a detective who worked with Coop, and someone I'd been dating for the past two years.

"I had a nice time last night," he said.

"So did I."

"Do you want to talk about it?"

"I thought we just did," I said.

"You know what I mean. Come on, Sloane, you know how I feel."

"And you know how *I* feel."

He sighed. "Every time I try to have the *us* talk, you shut down. I thought we'd decided to discuss taking the next step last night. I'm ready, and I thought you were too."

I stood for a moment, trying to decide what to say. I was getting to the place he was, but I wasn't there yet, and I didn't know how to tell him without it causing a problem.

"Sloane, you still there?" he asked.

"Yeah, I'm here."

"I wish you'd just quiet all the chaos in your head and give me an honest answer."

In a world full of men who would rather shoot themselves in the foot with a nail gun than discuss the current state of affairs in their relationship, Nick was the exception.

"You're right," I said. "We should talk it out."

"How about we meet tomorrow night for dinner, and you can tell me where you're at with everything?"

"All right. I can do that."

If only I had meant it.

We ended the call, and I walked to the sofa and sat down. The next step in the relationship consisted of cohabitating, which Nick had been pressuring me to do over the last several months. He was a *why not* person. I was the opposite. My entire life was made up of *whys*.

Why did we need to take the next step in our relationship?

Why couldn't things stay the same?

Things were good just the way they were.

Boo hopped off the couch, barking at the sliding glass door that opened to the back porch. I picked him up and peered outside. A large shadow moved between the pine trees, but night had blanketed the sky, making it too difficult to see. I flicked the porch light on and leaned over just enough to spot a female moose with her little one in tow. We exchanged curious glances, and then the pair turned and walked away.

I smiled, patted Boo on the head, and said, "It's all right. They're gone now."

My phone rang again. It was Marty.

"I've had you on my mind all day today," I said. "Is everything okay?"

"It's been a long day," he said, "and a tragic one at that."

"Why? What happened?"

He paused a moment, and then said, "It's one of the skiers, a local who comes here all the time. She's dead."

# CHAPTER 5

The morning sun shot its rays through the trees, melting away pieces of fallen snow from the weathered branches. I glanced at the temperature gauge on my car. It was a mere eight degrees outside, and I was en route to my office. My thoughts turned to the conversation I'd had with Marty the night before. The skier he'd spoken of had died instantly, running chest-first into a tree. To make matters worse, Marty had known her. They weren't close, but he'd regarded her as a friend.

The skier's name was Charlotte Halliwell. She was a celebrated, experienced skier known for all the medals she'd won in the sport when she was younger. Her senseless death was confusing. A tree should have been easy for her to avoid.

A married couple had found Charlotte's motionless body beneath the tree she'd crashed into and called Ski Patrol. When Patrol reached her, she wasn't breathing. CPR was administered, but the efforts were for naught. Nothing could be done to resuscitate her. She was dead.

I switched gears and thought about Nick and his desire to have an all-access pass to my life. I was certain we were better the way we were. The next step would change things, and I knew how he worked. One step always led to another … and another one after that. We'd move in together, and he'd push for marriage, and then what? Babies? Of course he wanted babies, but how many? I was in my late thirties. What if I couldn't provide them?

I parked in my usual spot, fumbled with my keys until I found the one to my office, and eyeballed Boo, who was sitting in the passenger seat, staring at the key ring like it was a fun, jingly toy he'd like to play with.

"Come on then," I said, reaching out for him.

Boo didn't move. He looked out the window, back at me, and then out the window again.

"Oh, it's not so bad," I said. "Come on, we'll hurry. I promise."

I snatched him up and made a mad dash for the door. With no appointments set for the day, walking around the office in my bare feet seemed like a wise choice. I squished my toes into the thick shag rug in the center of the room and breathed in the warmth of my office, all seventy-six degrees of it.

I made some hot chocolate, sat at my desk, and checked my phone messages. A woman named Audrey Halliwell gave her number and asked me to return her call. She didn't mention what she wanted, but I recognized the last name from my conversation with Marty the night before. I jotted her details down and dialed the number.

The call was answered on the second ring.

"Hello?" she said.

"This is Sloane Monroe. You called my office this morning. Is this Audrey Halliwell?"

"It is. Thanks for getting back to me so fast."

"What can I do for you?"

"I got your number from Mr. Langston, the man who manages the ski resort. I'd like to hire you."

"Sure. What can I do for you, Audrey?"

"I ... I'd like to meet in person instead of talking on the phone. Then we can discuss details, and you can tell me what you think."

She was being cryptic, but the tone in her voice aroused my curiosity.

"No problem," I said. "Why don't you stop by my office?"

"How soon can I come in?"

"Any time. I'm here all day."

"Perfect. I can be there in twenty minutes."

"Can I ask what it's regarding, at least?" I asked.

There was a long pause, and then she said, "It's about my sister. I think something bad happened to her."

# CHAPTER 6

Audrey entered my office wearing a tunic sweater. It was white this time instead of red, but just as tight as the other one she'd worn when I'd seen her at the ski resort the day before. Her eyes were puffy and red, and she looked like she hadn't slept much in the last twenty-four hours. She stared down at Boo, who was running circles around her feet, and managed to crack a smile.

"What a cutie," Audrey said. "Is she a Maltipoo?"

I shook my head. "*He's* a Westie."

Boo put his best paw forward. She couldn't resist and bent down to pick him up.

"I'm sorry," I said. "I usually don't bring him to the office when I meet with clients, but I hadn't planned on seeing anyone today."

"He's adorable and, honestly, just the kind of distraction I needed today."

She ran her fingers up and down his body and then placed him back on his bed. I motioned to the chair opposite my desk, and she sat down, resting her hands in her lap.

"Can I get you anything?" I asked. "Water? Tea? Coffee?"

"Gin?"

"Sorry, I don't usually keep gin at the office."

I was about to suggest wine when she said, "It's all right. It was my bad attempt at being funny. Water would be great."

I grabbed a bottle out of the mini fridge and handed it to her.

"I'm not even sure what I'm doing here," she said. "One minute, I think I'm going crazy, and the next, my suspicions seem valid enough to be here, talking to you."

"I recognize you from Wildwood," I said.

"I saw you with Mr. Langston. I really should apologize. It wasn't my intention to eavesdrop, but we were the only people in the café, and I overheard Marty say you were a private investigator."

"When I saw you, you looked like you were waiting for someone."

"I was."

She twisted the cap off the water bottle, gulped half of it down, and set it down on the desk. "The woman who died yesterday ..."

Her eyes filled with tears. I reached for a tissue and handed it to her.

"It's okay," I said. "Take your time. There's no rush."

We sat in silence for a minute, and then she wiped her nose and said, "The woman who died was my sister."

I thought of my own sister, and flashes of memories from the past filtered through my mind like a slideshow in slow motion. I took a deep breath and tried to focus.

"I'm sorry," I said.

She grabbed another tissue from the box and dabbed her eyes. "Let me just ... I need a minute to get myself together."

I nodded. "When you're ready, why don't we start from the beginning?"

"Sure. You mind if I smoke?"

I did mind—a lot, in fact. But I also knew a cigarette might be the calm she needed right now. I managed to find a small glass dish in one of my drawers and handed it to her.

Audrey reached into her bag and pulled out a cigarette. She rested it on the edge of her lips, cupped the lighter in her hands and lit up. She took a long drag and cocked her head to one side, attempting to spew the stream of smoke away from me. It didn't work, and I did my best to sit there, acting as though it did.

"I went to Wildwood yesterday to meet my sister for lunch," she said. "We'd talked on the phone the night before, and she said she had something important to tell me."

"Did she give you any idea of what it was?"

She shook her head. "She said she needed my advice and suggested we talk over lunch once she'd finished skiing. I was sitting there in the resort café, irritated, thinking she had lost track of time. I had somewhere else to be, so after you left, I asked the front desk if I could leave her a note. That's when Marty called me into his office."

"What did he say?"

"He said she'd had an accident. But it doesn't make any sense."

"You've experienced a shock. I'm sure nothing makes sense right now."

She took another drag from the cigarette and smashed the butt into the plate. "You don't understand. *Everyone* assumes it was an accident because it *looks* like an accident. What if it wasn't?"

Audrey looked me in the eye, waiting for me to react to her theory.

"On the phone you said you thought something bad had happened to her," I said. "What did you mean?"

"I don't know. I can't decide whether I'm just confused, or whether my suspicions are valid. It's hard to separate my head from my heart right now, you know?"

I knew the feeling all too well.

She leaned forward and tapped a finger on the edge of the desk, thinking.

"Oh, to hell with this," she said. "I'm here. I may as well say it like it is, and if you think I'm a nut job, oh well. But I need to get it off my chest."

"All right. Go ahead."

"I don't believe my sister's death was an accident. In fact, I *know* it wasn't. Charlotte was murdered, and I want to hire you to find out who did it."

# CHAPTER 7

Audrey's blatant allegation piqued my interest, causing me to wonder what made her feel the way she did.

"What do you know about my sister's death?" Audrey asked.

"Not much," I said. "I know she ran into a tree while skiing."

"She did. I'm not buying it being an accident, though."

"Have you told anyone else about your suspicions?"

"I talked to the cops about my theory last night. They blew me off, treating me like I was creating alternate theories about her death as a way to cope with my grief. But my sister wasn't some newbie. She started skiing at the age of two, and she's skied that particular run almost every day since Wildwood opened. It was her favorite. She knew it well."

"I don't mean any disrespect," I said, "but even experienced skiers crash now and then."

"Charlotte went to the World Championship twice before she turned twenty. She has a silver medal, for heaven's sake."

Interesting.

Audrey pointed out the window. "Look out there."

I looked outside, seeing nothing of particular interest.

Maybe Audrey *was* a little crazy.

"Take a good look," she said. "Nothing but blue skies all week. Now you tell me, how does someone with my sister's experience run into a tree on a clear day?"

"I don't know. Did your sister take any medications?"

She shook her head. "I don't think so. She was the type of person who preferred herbal remedies for any ailments she might have had."

"What about injuries? Has she ever had any other skiing accidents?"

"She broke her arm a couple of times when she was a teenager and broke her leg once."

Her eyes flashed like she was recalling a memory.

"What is it?" I asked.

"When we were kids, she almost died."

"How?"

"Charlotte fell out of the back of our dad's truck. She hit her head on a boulder and it knocked her unconscious. When she came to, she said she had died, and that she'd been to the *other side* … you know, long tunnel, bright light, people dressed in white robes, and stuff. It was a long time ago, though. I called her doctor this morning. Charlotte was in perfect health the day she died."

"You said she wanted your advice. Any idea what she needed to discuss with you?"

She fidgeted with the bottom of her sweater. It rolled up at the ends, and she smoothed it back down with her fingers, and then she repeated the ritual. "Charlotte didn't say what she wanted to talk to me about. I guess I'll never know now."

"What was her tone of voice like when she called you last? Did she act like something was wrong?"

"She sounded nervous, and Charlotte doesn't get nervous. Not about much, anyway. She always had a glass-half-full approach to life, even when she had a good reason not to."

In my line of work I'd learned sometimes the aloof, calm types had the most to hide.

"What did she do for work?" I asked.

"She was a real estate agent. She liked her job. She thought of transferring to another agency, but she never did."

"Any idea why she considered a change?"

"Money, I guess. She told me another agency had offered her a better commission if she transferred to their office."

"What about her coworkers?" I asked. "Any problems there?"

She shrugged. "As far as I know, she got along with everyone."

"Did anyone else know about the offer she received to switch to another office?"

"Her partner, Vicki, and her assistant, Bridget. I assumed the three of them would go together. They worked as a team."

"So if there wasn't a problem with work, then why do you suspect foul play?"

Audrey crossed her arms in front of her. "I want you to check out her fiancé, Parker Stanton, or *ex*-fiancé, I should say."

"Why him?"

"A couple of months ago, she broke off their engagement."

I took a sip of my hot chocolate. It was cold and no longer suitable to drink, but spitting it back into the cup seemed like an indecorous thing to do, so I swallowed, hard, and slid the mug to the side.

"What was the reason for the breakup?" I asked.

"Parker spends a lot of time away from her. He works for his family and travels back and forth to New York a lot. At the beginning of their relationship, he was only away three or four days a week, but toward the end, he'd be gone most of the week."

"Is that why she ended it?"

"I think so."

"Didn't she talk to you about their relationship?"

"Sometimes. At first it didn't bother her that he was gone. She saw it as a temporary setback. We went on a girls' trip last month, just the two of us. Charlotte called Parker several times over the weekend, but he didn't answer. Then on Sunday night, he called to say he'd been having phone problems and hadn't received any of her messages, which was clearly a load of crap. After a few minutes on the phone he made some lame excuse about how he needed to go meet with his dad and abruptly ended the call … while she was still talking."

"How did Charlotte react?"

"She broke off the engagement as soon as he returned home."

"How did Parker take it?" I asked.

"He was shocked. Parker's the type of guy who thinks he can do anything and get away with it. He called, sent gifts, and even booked two tickets to Hawaii for a weekend getaway. He said he would do anything to keep her. All he wanted was a second chance."

"And did she give him one?"

"She did not. She sent him a text message saying she didn't ever want to see or hear from him again."

It made me wonder what else may have been going on in the relationship to upset her. Charlotte could have ended it because of his lack of consideration, and possibly even over suspicions that he wasn't doing what he said he was, but I assumed there was more to it—things she hadn't told her sister.

"What do you think of Parker?" I asked.

"He's a spoiled rich kid who spends his life doing a minimal amount of his daddy's grunt work and the rest of his time playing. In my opinion the only reason he involves himself in the business in the first place is to try to convince everyone he's his own man. But everyone knows he's daddy's lackey."

*Wow. Tell me how you really feel.*

"Don't get me wrong," she continued. "Parker played nice. He treated my sister like a princess, showering her with gifts, showing her what it was like to have *real* money. It may have worked with other women, but not with her. Charlotte didn't care about Parker's family's net worth."

"I appreciate your honesty."

"It's just ... I've always felt there was something *off* about Parker."

"Off, how?"

"I don't know how to explain it. The guy gives me the creeps."

The way her face wrinkled when she said the word *creeps* was like someone who'd tasted something awful that they never wanted to eat again.

"Define *creeps*," I said.

"He's the only man I've ever met who can sweet-talk his way out of anything."

Until Charlotte dumped him. Still, it didn't make him creepy. It made him a douche.

Audrey slumped back in the chair.

"Anything else I should know about Parker?" I asked.

"Yeah, one thing. He called me."

"When?"

"A few weeks ago. He wanted me to help him get things back on track with my sister. I told him he could go to hell."

"What did he say?"

"He flipped out and said he'd get Charlotte back with or without my help."

"And you think he's capable of murder?"

"He thinks he's above the law."

"That doesn't make him a murderer," I said.

"I know something's not right. I can feel it. You will help me, won't you?"

I tapped my pen on the desk, considering everything she'd told me. I'd take the case. I wasn't sure if I believed the allegation about her sister's death being a murder, but it was worth checking out.

"I'll look into it," I said, "but you need to understand, I might not find anything."

"If you don't, at least I'll be able to put my suspicions to rest."

Her phone buzzed. She removed it from her bag and clicked on the text message she'd just received. She rolled her eyes and shoved the phone back into her purse.

"Everything okay?" I asked.

She shook her head. "An autopsy was ordered, but they told me it could take weeks before all of the results come in. So I ordered a private autopsy, hoping I could speed things along. The medical examiner's office just got back to me, saying they need a day or two before Charlotte can be processed, and that's just the beginning. Who knows how long the results will take? I had no idea it was so complicated."

It wasn't, not always.

"I might be able to help. Let me make some calls, and I'll get back to you. In the meantime, I'd like to take a look at your sister's place. Do you have a way to get in?"

Audrey pulled a key ring holding three keys out of her purse. She twisted one off and handed it to me. "Her address is 1233 Powderhorn Street. Let me know if you find anything."

# CHAPTER 8

Charlotte Halliwell was a celebrity in Park City. Locals adored her athletic achievements, and tourists for her unyielding and tireless effort in finding them the perfect vacation home of their dreams. Her slogan: *You can ski in, but you won't want to ski out,* made an impression on people. Proving her death wasn't an accident wouldn't be easy.

I was running late. Too late. I sized up my shower, but decided there was no time for a quickie. On my way out, I caught my reflection in the mirror. My long, dark hair looked decent, but my makeup needed refreshing. I spruced myself up and then dashed out the door.

It was one minute past seven in the evening when I arrived at Moll's Tavern. I walked in and looked around, but there was no sign of Nick, who, unlike me, ran on his own time schedule. I waved myself past the hostess, ordered a drink at the bar, and then sat at my favorite table—a dimly lit booth at the back, which offered the most privacy.

I sat there waiting, trying to relax and concentrate on my drink, a dirty martini with extra olives, but I couldn't tear my eyes away from the haphazard arrangement of silverware on the table in front of me. The spoon to the left of the knife and the salad and dinner forks to the right. I gathered them up, reorganizing the flatware in its correct position, and then leaned back, amazed at the satisfaction I felt from a little silverware organization.

OCD was more than a singular disorder. There were five subtypes: contamination obsessions with cleaning compulsions, obsessions without visible compulsions, hoarding, harm obsessions with checking compulsions, and symmetry obsessions with ordering compulsions—the one I had just suffered.

"Couldn't resist, could you?" a male voice said.

I looked up. "You're late."

Nick winked. "No more than usual."

"About ten minutes, but who's counting?"

He glanced at my martini. "I see you went ahead."

I held my glass up high and smiled. "I did. Cheers!"

Nick was dressed in a gray button-down shirt and dark denim jeans, which looked great on his stocky, five-foot-ten body. He had a hint of a five o'clock shadow, which complemented his brown buzz cut. Aside from the lack of a uniform, he looked like he belonged in the military.

The owner of the restaurant rounded the corner, saw me, and her eyes lit up. She was a broad-sized Irish woman in her fifties, with freckles from head to toe.

She shuffled over to the table and gave me a side hug. "Sloane, how wonderful to see you."

"And you, Claire," I said.

She tipped her head toward my drink. "How's the martini?"

"Perfect. How's business?"

"I have no complaints. You want your usual?"

I nodded.

"I'll tell your waitress," she said, "if I can find the silly thing. She's new. As useful as a lighthouse on a bog, that one."

"Is anyone at all interested in what I want?" Nick asked.

Claire laughed and shifted her attention from me to him.

She patted him on the arm. "Give us girls time to catch up, and we'll get you all taken care of, all right?"

We chatted for another minute, and she walked away, forgetting Nick in the process.

Nick sized up my martini like he wanted to frisk it. "She didn't even ask if I wanted a drink."

I waved the waitress over to our table. "He'll have a Bulleit Neat."

"A bull … what?" she asked.

Claire wasn't the patient type. If the new hire planned on making it, she didn't have long to master the drink list.

"A bourbon on the rocks," I said. "Ask the bartender. He'll know."

She took our food order and walked away.

Nick grabbed my hand and looked straight at me. "Now, where were we?"

"Somewhere between OCD and what we did today, I think."

"Right," he said. "You first."

"What do you know so far about the accident at Wildwood?"

"Same as you, I'll bet. The woman crashed near the bottom of the ski run and died of blunt-force trauma from the looks of it. Why do you ask?"

"Her sister, Audrey Halliwell, came to see me today."

"What about?"

"The accident, or should I say, alleged accident. She hired me to look into it."

The smile on his face vanished. "What do you mean *alleged?*"

"She thinks there's a chance her sister's death wasn't an accident."

The waitress returned with Nick's drink and our salads.

"Another martini?" she asked.

I nodded, handing her my glass.

Nick took a swig of his drink. "We already know what happened."

"You know what you *think* happened. Charlotte's sister suspects otherwise."

"Based on what?"

"Charlotte Halliwell was an experienced skier. And before you chime in, I already know what you're going to say. That, in itself, doesn't prove foul play, and you're right."

"You know family members don't always think rationally after losing a loved one," he said.

"I do, and right now, I don't know what to think. But I don't see how poking around a little can hurt."

He leaned back and grabbed his drink. "You didn't take this case because of Gabrielle, did you?"

I picked at my salad and tried my best not to stab it.

Nick reached over and wrapped his hand around my wrist. "I shouldn't have said that. I'm sorry."

"Don't worry about it. It's no big deal."

"She was your sister. What happened to her was … well … awful. It *is* a big deal."

"That's not why I took the case."

It was true, for the most part.

The waitress returned with our food, and for a couple of minutes, we ate in silence.

"So, what's the plan of attack?" Nick asked.

"The usual. I'll talk to people she knew, check out the ex-boyfriend, take a look at her place, and see what turns up."

"Let me know what you find out," he said.

I nodded. "The sister is also paying for a second autopsy."

"Maybe that's a good thing. When it comes back with no indication of foul play, hopefully she'll accept it and move on."

It seemed logical, but I wasn't so sure it would.

Nick's cell phone vibrated. He looked at the screen, sighed, and then answered it. "Everything all right?"

He paused, listening to the caller on the other line, and said, "Sure, I'll be right there."

He ended the call and set his drink down on the table.

"What's happened?" I asked.

"I hate to cut out on you on date night, but there's a homicide I've been asked to assist on. A tourist found out his wife was cheating on him with one of the other guys in their group. He went to the guy's hotel room, found them kissing on the balcony, and tossed the guy over the side."

"Love goes by haps; Some Cupid kills with arrows, some with traps."

Nick raised a brow. "What's that?"

"Shakespeare."

"Nice. Well, have another drink for me and then grab a taxi home. If I finish at a decent time, I'll head to your place."

He leaned in, brushed his lips across mine, and walked away, and though I was sorry to see him go, there was one positive in him leaving. The conversation he wanted to have about our relationship had successfully been postponed.

# CHAPTER 9

The next morning I exercised my options and phoned a friend.

"I'm calling in a favor, Maddie," I said.

"Big one or little one?"

"I'm not sure yet. It depends on what you find. I have a new case, and it's a bit on the unusual side."

"Ahh, my favorite kind."

Maddie had been my closest friend for many years. She was also a well-known medical examiner who sometimes traveled the country giving lectures on recent breakthroughs in forensic pathology.

The phone made a distinct cracking noise. At first, I chocked it up to a bad connection, but then I realized it was just Maddie grinding on the wad of gum she was chewing.

"Did you hear about the skiing accident at Wildwood a couple days ago?" I asked.

"It was mentioned on the news this morning, but I was running around the house, so I only caught bits and pieces."

I filled her in on the details.

She popped a bubble into the phone.

At times, it was hard to believe her IQ exceeded mine.

"What do you think about the sister's theory?" Maddie asked. "It sounds kind of far out, you know?"

"I believe she wants it to be true, and since there's a disgruntled ex-fiancé, I have a good place to start, at least. If I turn up nothing, I turn up nothing. I still get paid either way."

Maddie laughed. "Where's the victim, and how much time do I have to look her over?"

"They've transferred Charlotte to the funeral home. And it would be great if you could get to her today or tomorrow. Let's just say 'weeks' don't register in Audrey Halliwell's vocabulary right now."

"Not the patient type, eh?"

"Not in the least," I said.

"You two should get along famously, then."

# CHAPTER 10

Marty stood at the front desk, peering out into the parking lot like he was in a trance. His eyes had deep-set bags under them, and although he looked tired, he did his best to muster up a smile when I walked through the door.

"Thanks for seeing me," I said.

"I always have time for you." He gestured toward his office. "Let's sit for a minute."

I followed him to the office and sat on a leather chair that looked like it had been designed more for looks and less for comfort.

"I wanted to talk to you about Charlotte Halliwell," I said.

He nodded. "When Audrey asked for your number, I expected you'd be coming around."

"I met with her yesterday. She's not handling her sister's death well. Not that I blame her."

Marty shook his head. "It's a shame, really. Charlotte was such a sweet girl, and I've known her grandfather for years. He was a big supporter of mine when I ran for mayor."

"Audrey believes Charlotte's death wasn't an accident. Did you know that?"

Marty's eyes widened. He leaned all the way back in his chair, pondering what I'd just said.

"I don't understand," he said. "What happened here was a tragedy, a horrible accident. What proof does she have to suggest otherwise?"

"Maybe nothing, but she's hired me to look into it."

"Do you think she's just in shock and doesn't want to accept what happened to her sister?"

I shrugged. "Maybe."

"I don't know what to say. What can I do?"

"Can I take a look at the crash site?"

"I doubt it would do much good."

"I'd still like to see it."

"All right," he said.

"Did Charlotte keep a locker?"

He nodded.

"I'd like to take a look at it too," I said. "I'll text Audrey and ask her if she'd like me to gather up what's inside and bring it to her."

"Good idea."

"And I have one final request. I'd like to talk to your staff, to anyone working a couple of days ago, and see if they'd interacted with Charlotte before she headed out to go skiing."

Marty ran his forefinger and thumb across his jaw and stared at a picture on the wall—a skier plowing his way through a thicket of trees. "Can you hold off on talking to my staff for now?"

It wasn't the response I'd hoped for, but two out of three requests wasn't a bad start. "I suppose I could wait. It sure would help me, though."

"I'd like to keep your investigation under wraps for the moment. The resort hasn't been open long, and I'd rather not have a bunch of unfavorable stories floating around about this place before there's proof that Charlotte died any other way than accidentally. It's been tough enough as it is. You understand Sloane, don't you?"

I was disappointed, but I could see where he was coming from. We finished our conversation, and Marty escorted me out of his office.

The sun peeked through the trees, trying to convince me it was warmer outside than it seemed. I bundled up so much I resembled the Stay Puft Marshmallow Man, but the pricey snow gear I was dressed, designed to keep me warm, was only doing a half-ass job at best. Marty threw a thick, black jacket over his suit, changed out of his dress shoes into a pair of snow boots, and we were off.

We took the lift most of the way down, and then trudged through the snow on foot to the place the accident had occurred. To show respect for the place Charlotte died, Marty had decided to close that particular slope for a few days. Without anyone on it, a new batch of snow had formed over the old, giving it a fresh, renewed appearance that made it feel like nothing had happened there at all.

Marty stopped and spread his arms to the side. "Well, here we are."

"It's so quiet and peaceful. It's hard to believe she died here."

"Snow groomers came around last night and flattened it all out."

I turned my attention to the tree. Staring at it now, I found it odd that she ran into it at all. From the center of the run, it stood some twenty plus yards away. There were a few other trees in the immediate vicinity, but it was sparse at best. To crash into it, she would have gone way off course.

"Could there have been any problems with her equipment?" I asked.

"Everything was checked after the accident. It all looked fine."

"And no one was around to see it happen?"

"Not a soul until she was found. It's the hardest course, so it's not as widely used as the others."

I threw my hands up in the air. "I guess I'm done, then. Sorry to drag you out here with me."

We returned to the lodge and Marty retrieved the key to Charlotte's locker.

He handed it to me and pointed. "It's through those doors. Number one thirty-three."

"You don't need to come with me?"

"I can't. It's ahh ... the women's locker room."

"Oh, okay. Had she rented it just for the day, or longer?"

He shook his head. "Charlotte skied here two or three times a week, sometimes more. I gave her the locker for the season."

I walked into the locker room and found the number I needed. The locker was separated into two compartments. The top shelf contained a pair of jeans. I checked the pockets. They were empty. Behind the pants I found a black studded belt, a pink sweater, white socks, and a pair of black boots. Nothing unusual there. I moved on to the second shelf. It contained an oversized handbag. I removed it and pulled open the magnetic clasp at the top. Inside was what appeared to be a real estate book of some kind. I flipped it open. It had a pocket on the left containing a small monthly planner with the names and numbers of all of Charlotte's appointments. I flipped to the back of the book and checked the other pocket. It was empty. Other than the planner, the bag contained a wallet, a makeup bag, and a cell phone. I pulled out the phone. There were three calls and two text messages. Two of the calls were from an appointment she'd missed. A husband and wife with the last name of Duchene called to find out why she was late and then tried back a second time thirty minutes later. The third call was from Charlotte's assistant, Bridget, who said the Duchenes had called Vicki when Charlotte failed to show up for the appointment.

Next I checked the text messages. Both were from Parker Stanton. The first arrived at ten fifteen on the morning she died. It said: *I miss you. Call me.* The second message followed a few hours later: *Why are you ignoring me, Charlotte? Don't play games with me! I've given you space. You can't keep avoiding me like this. I'm heading to the lodge. We WILL talk this out.*

I shoved Charlotte's cell phone inside my jacket pocket and took the key back to Marty.

"Any luck?" he said.

"Hard to say right now."

I didn't want to worry him unnecessarily. I hadn't found any incriminating evidence and decided a couple of angry text messages weren't worth sounding the alarm.

Not yet.

# CHAPTER 11

I woke the next day to the sound of my cell phone ringing. It was Nick.

"Hey," I said.

"I just came from the chief's office," he said. "He wants to see you."

"What about?"

"I think you know the answer to that question already, don't you? News travels fast."

I recalled a time as a child when my mother had forced me to sit at the table for hours after I'd refused to eat the last few carrots on my plate. I didn't care how long I sat there or how stale the carrots became. The minutes ticked by, and I didn't budge. I wasn't going to eat it no matter how much she coaxed me. Driving to the station, I had a similar feeling of disdain. Except this time, I was an adult, and it was my duty to go whether I liked it or not.

A year earlier when Wade Sheppard was named the new chief of police in Park City, he had called me, suggesting I learn the ropes and become a cop. I politely declined. After establishing my own successful business, I couldn't imagine starting over again and subjecting myself to rigorous training just to be put on beat, hoping for a chance to one day be made a detective. I would have started at the bottom of the barrel as a rookie who was much older than everyone else. Besides, I preferred life on my own terms without all the red tape. Sure, I stepped on a toe or two now and then, but I only answered to one person: *me*. Freedom like that wasn't worth giving up, at any price.

Coop was perched by the entrance when I walked into the station, hunched over the coffee machine. He tipped his head at me when I walked in but didn't smile.

"Miss Monroe," he said.

"Coop," I said.

"Hear you got yourself a new case."

"I did."

"Do yourself a favor. See it for what it really is and quit while you're still ahead."

Before I had the chance to respond, Sheppard stepped outside his office and glared at me. "Sloane, my office, now."

As I walked toward Sheppard's office, Coop's booming voice sounded off in the background. "Good luck in there. You'll need it."

Sheppard's office was in its usual disheveled state. The drawers to the file cabinet were open to various degrees, and files were strewn across his desk. In the center of the desk on top of a heap of paperwork rested the day's paper. The chief paced back and forth and then grabbed the paper, hurling it in my direction.

"Care to explain to me what in the hell this is about?" he asked.

I picked it up, glancing at the front page. Plastered above the fold was a picture of Charlotte and the headline: LOCAL GIRL DIES IN TRAGIC ACCIDENT.

I stared at it for a moment. Charlotte was a beauty. She had straight red hair that fell just above her chin line, and the bluest eyes I'd ever seen.

"Well?" he asked.

I tossed the paper back on the desk. "I'm not sure what you want me to say. It looks like an article about what happened at Wildwood. What's the problem?"

He pushed the paper back in my direction and stabbed at the article with his finger. "Read it. All of it."

Given his icy glare and current demeanor, part of me didn't want to.

I did anyway.

The article contained the usual information. It cited the date of Charlotte's death and where it had taken place, followed by a brief mention of her earlier career as a professional skier. It sounded like the usual humdrum … until I reached the end:

*The cause of death, while accidental, has not yet been determined. Audrey Halliwell, sister of the deceased, had this to say. "I don't believe my sister's death was an accident. She was an experienced skier. I tried explaining this to the local police, but they didn't take me seriously, and in my opinion, there's some kind of cover-up going on to hide what really happened: foul play. The cops don't seem to care, leaving me no choice but to make sure justice is served myself by hiring my own private investigator to do the job they're obviously not interested in doing."*

I folded the paper and placed it back on the desk, resisting the urge to crawl beneath it.

"Tell me you're not involved with this unbalanced woman," he said.

I looked at him.

"Aww, hell," he said. "I knew it. I tried talking to Nick about it, and he skipped out on me without answering the question."

"Audrey Halliwell believes there's more to Charlotte's death than a simple accident."

Beads of sweat pooled around his forehead, and I braced for impact. "More to *what*? How does a damned accident make the front page as a possible homicide?"

"I know what you're thinking, but she hired me to do a job, and I intend to see it through, whatever the outcome. It doesn't mean she's right."

"I'm asking you to drop the case."

He wasn't *asking* anything.

"I can't," I said. "Not yet, anyway."

"Fine. I'm *telling* you to drop it. My phone hasn't stopped ringing today, and now I've got reporters crawling all over me for an interview about what *really* happened to this woman."

"I didn't speak to the media."

"But your client did," he said. "She's a loose cannon who's struggling with her sister's death. Smearing this department's reputation in the media won't change the fact that her sister is dead."

His mouth snapped shut. I assumed it was because he'd realized the way his words had just cut through the air, like he was harsh and without compassion.

"I'll talk to her," I said. "I really didn't know she planned on speaking out. I thought she was going to allow me time to look into what happened to see if there's any merit to her assumptions."

His expression relaxed a little. "When you talk to her, will you tell her you can't proceed? It was an accident, Sloane. Nothing more."

"If it *was* an accident, you shouldn't have a problem if I check it out."

He clenched his hand into a fist and slammed it down on the desk. The coffee in his cup sloshed into the air, sending hot liquid in every direction.

"Let it go! I'm giving you an order."

"I don't want this to cause a rift between us," I said, "but I don't work for you."

He looked at me and shook his head, disappointed. "We're done here. Get out of my office."

I wanted to stay until we smoothed things over, but he was far too angry. I walked out, closing the office door behind me. Coop stood a few feet away with a couple of his buddies. They snickered when I passed like a pack of immature jackals.

"What do you think?" Coop said. "Shall I call the tree in for questioning, Sloane?"

The two officers next to him erupted in laughter, which only added fuel to his fire.

"Yes, uh, Mr. Tree," he said. "May I ask where you were between the hours of say ten a.m. and noon? And you didn't move all day, you say?"

I thrust my hands against the front door and headed outside.

From the looks of it, the chief wasn't the only laughing stock.

# CHAPTER 12

The real estate office of Ellis and Marshall sat smack dab in the middle of Old Town, right next to one of the transit bus stops. Skiers gussied up like big, puffy balls stood with their skis in tow, waiting in anticipation for the bus to make its rounds. Next stop for them, the slopes. Next stop for me: a chat with Charlotte's real estate partner.

A flat-screen television with an on-screen display of homes ridiculously out of my price range drew me in when I entered, enticing me to live the fantasy. Behind it was a wall full of featured homes. One in particular stood out, and I couldn't resist the urge to lean in and take a closer look.

"It's a beauty, isn't it?" a woman's voice said.

I turned. An older woman in her mid-fifties wearing bright red lipstick stood next to me. Her ash-blond, coarse, shoulder-length hair looked like she'd stuck her finger in a light socket and had forgotten to brush it out.

"Oh, I'm just looking," I said. "I already have a house."

She grabbed the photo I had been admiring, taking it off the wall. "This one's a real charmer, and just reduced too."

*Reduced to a mere million and a half.*

*No, thank you.*

"Deer Valley is one of the nicest areas in Park City," she said. "And this little beauty won't stay on the market for long."

The more she talked, the more she reminded me of a starving piranha, with the exception of one thing—there was something in her tired, watery eyes that suggested otherwise, a sadness I assumed was going around the office.

"I'm looking for Vicki Novak," I said.

She extended her hand. "You found her. It's nice to meet you. And you are?"

I gave her my name.

"I'm not working today," she said. "I just stopped by the office for a few minutes, but I haven't seen any other agents around since I got here. I'm guessing they're all out working or taking some personal time like I have been this week. Anyway, since I appear to be the only one here at the moment, if there is something I can do for you, we can talk in my office."

She gestured to the stairs on the right.

"Sure," I said.

I followed her upstairs. When we entered the room, the first thing I noticed was the framed photo sitting on top of her desk. It was a picture of Vicki and Charlotte with their arms around one another.

"So, what can I do for you today?" she asked.

"I'd like to talk to you about your real estate partner," I said.

She frowned and folded her arms. "Oh, I see. Do you work for the paper? Because I don't have anything to—"

"I'm not a reporter," I said. "Were you and Charlotte partners long?"

"Well, let's see, about five years, give or take. It's terrible, you know? I still can't believe she's gone."

"I'm sorry."

She smoothed a hand across her wet eyelid. "I can't stop thinking about it. I can't sleep. I can't eat. It's like this pit in my stomach that won't go away."

"How was your relationship with Charlotte before she died?"

"Forgive my rudeness, but you still haven't told me who you are, and you ask a lot of questions for someone who isn't a reporter. Are you with the police?"

I shook my head. "I'm a friend of Charlotte's sister, Audrey."

"That still doesn't explain why you're here."

"Audrey hired me to look into Charlotte's death."

Vicki had a stupefied look on her face like I'd just administered a shock to her system. I waited a moment for my words to sink in.

"I don't understand," she said.

"Audrey suspects what happened to Charlotte wasn't an accident," I said. "Haven't you seen today's paper?"

"I ... haven't kept up on much of anything over the last few days. We were told it was a skiing accident."

"It might be. In the meantime, I'd like your help."

Tears trickled down her face. "I'm sorry. I'm usually a lot more together than this."

"It's no problem. Take your time."

"I don't know how much help I can be, but I'll try."

"Is it true the two of you planned a transfer to another agency?"

"We discussed it, but no decision was ever made."

"Why make the switch at all?" I asked.

"Charlotte felt the time was right. A new agency had opened in town, and they offered a better commission split. She said we should move before the other real estate agents swooped in and we would miss our chance."

"How did you feel about going to work for another agency?"

"I was the one who convinced her to stay where we're at."

"Why?"

"We made a name for ourselves at this office, and between the two of us, we made plenty of money. I worried about what would happen if we made the switch and it didn't work out."

"Couldn't you have just come back here?" I asked.

"A few months ago one of the other top-selling agents moved to a different office. She didn't get along with everyone there, and when she asked our broker to take her back, he said he'd already moved an agent into her office, but that wasn't true. He took it personally when she left. He felt betrayed. I worried it could happen to us too. Park City isn't the smallest city, but it's small enough."

"Can you think of anyone who wanted to harm her?"

She bit down on the side of her lip, thinking. "Mmmph, no, not really. She was a likable person. Everyone got along with her."

"What about Parker Stanton? What do you think of him?"

"He always seemed like a nice guy. Well, most of the time."

"And the other times?"

"He's a guy. You know how guys are. Sometimes they're sweet and other times they're ahh … well, in Parker's case, he could be a little aggressive."

"Are you saying he was violent?" I asked.

"I liked him, but Parker and Charlotte had a few flare-ups here and there."

"Can you give me an example?"

"One time Charlotte and I had made plans to meet with a high-profile client who had flown in to tour homes with us. Right before we left the office, Parker called and said he needed her or wanted to talk to her. I don't recall all the specifics. Charlotte said she was tied up, and she'd get back to him as soon as we returned. Parker wasn't satisfied with her answer."

"What happened?" I asked.

"When we came back to the office, he was waiting for her in the parking lot. I'll never forget the look on her face when we drove in. It was like she knew she was going to catch hell from him, and she sure did. Once her car door opened, Parker hustled over, grabbed her by the arm, and yanked her back to his car."

"And then?"

"I'm not sure. I remember she left with him, though. I texted her to see if she was all right, and she said everything was fine, so I thought the way I'd perceived him that day was worse than it actually was. But a few days later, they broke up."

"How would you define your relationship with Charlotte?"

She glanced at the picture on her desk. "We were in real estate school together. When we graduated, she started selling right away, but I had trouble closing deals consistently and struggled to make a good income during some months. I actually considered quitting the business altogether. Charlotte found out and suggested we team up. We've worked together ever since."

I stood. "Thanks for the information. I appreciate you taking the time to talk with me. I'd also like to speak with Charlotte's assistant, Bridget. Is she here today?"

"Bridget hasn't shown up for work since the accident happened. I've tried reaching her by phone, but I can't get an answer. One of the other assistants in the office said she thought Bridget was moving in with her boyfriend. You can talk to Jack Montgomery. He might have more information. And if he doesn't, his secretary should know something."

"And Jack is?" I asked.

"He's our broker. His office is downstairs, second one on the right."

# CHAPTER 13

Jack Montgomery was sitting at his desk with an assortment of papers in one hand and a half-eaten cookie in the other. His door was wide open, but I knocked anyway.

"Excuse me," I said. "Mr. Montgomery?"

He set the pile of paperwork on the desk and looked up at me. "Hello, and you are?"

I offered my name. He leaned forward, extending his hand.

"I hoped to get an address from you for Charlotte Halliwell's assistant," I said.

He looked straight ahead at a plaque, studying it for a moment. From my vantage point, I could see a few names engraved on it: Charlotte, Jack, Vicki, and two others. The accolade read: *Top Agents of the Year.*

"Whatever information you need can be acquired through my secretary," he said.

It was what I expected him to say, but I wasn't ready to excuse myself yet.

"Were you aware Charlotte Halliwell wanted to transfer to another agency?" I asked.

He squirmed in his chair like a schoolboy waiting for the recess bell to ring.

"She's dead now," he said. "I don't see why it matters."

"Why wouldn't it? She was the best-selling agent in the office, wasn't she?"

"Not just the office, in all of Summit County. Her death is a huge loss, to everyone."

The *loss* he spoke of sounded like it was coming more from a place of profitability than sympathy.

"Charlotte was unparalleled, a one-of-a-kind in our industry," he said. "I've never seen an agent with the same drive and ambition as she had."

"With her track record, I imagine the other agents were jealous of her success."

"Possibly. If they were, I didn't know anything about it. There's nothing wrong with a bit of friendly competition, but we're all friends here."

"Why do you think she wanted to work for another agency?" I asked.

"She didn't. Why are you asking? Why is it so important to you?"

"I heard Charlotte planned to transfer to another agency."

"That's horse shit. Who told you that?"

"Her sister," I said.

"I don't know why she's running around spreading rumors like she is, but she doesn't know what she's talking about."

"Agents transfer to different agencies all the time. Why is it so hard for you to believe it isn't something she would have considered?"

He glared at me. "I don't have time to answer any more of your questions."

"There's no need for you to get defensive."

He leaned forward in his chair, crossing his arms in front of him. "I don't know why you've decided to come to my office and make all these wild accusations, but I'm understaffed this week—this office has been deserted. I have work to do."

A woman entered and handed a stack of papers to Jack. She saw the look on his face and backed out of the room, closing the door behind her.

"If I can just get Bridget's address, I'll be on my way," I said.

He shook his head. "You can't, and it's time for you to go."

I honored his wishes and left, certain of one thing: Jack Montgomery was lying about Charlotte.

But why?

# CHAPTER 14

Audrey checked in with me the following afternoon to ask if I had anything new to report. I shared what little information I'd gathered, including my recent altercation with the police chief.

"I didn't mean to get you into any trouble," she said, "but those smug detectives didn't seem to give a crap when they were talking to me."

"I understand how they made you feel," I said, "but I need you to give me a heads-up before you do things like talk to reporters, all right? I went into the chief's office with no knowledge of what you'd said, which left me unprepared to handle it. I was hoping he'd agree to be my ally, to share any information he receives. Now, there's no way he'll let me in."

"Guess I didn't think before I spoke."

"I want to help you, and I will do everything I can, but I need you to see what we're doing as a team effort. When it comes to your sister, I need to know to whom you're talking and what you're saying. I cannot work with you otherwise."

She was silent for a moment. "I suppose I owe you an apology. When those reporters got in my face, I lost it."

"You've been through a lot," I said. "It's understandable."

"Is there anything I can do to make things better?"

"I need an address for Parker Stanton. Do you know where he lives?"

"I do. He has a house off Silver Lake Drive in Deer Valley. It's the second house on the left. He also has an investment property downtown in Salt Lake City that he stays at sometimes, when it's not occupied. I think he rents it out most of the time, though. It's called Lakewood or Lockwood. I'm not sure about the unit number."

"You'd mentioned that Parker was gone during the week before the breakup. Any idea what his schedule is now?"

"I'm not sure what he's up to these days."

I ended the call with one thought: it was time to find out.

# CHAPTER 15

The lights inside the house at 112 Silver Lake Drive were off when I arrived. I situated my car behind a broken lamppost down the street and sat and waited. I'd driven over hoping to find the lights on, confirmation Parker was in town. I had some time to kill, so I decided I'd wait for a while and see if he turned up.

It wasn't long before my thoughts turned to my sister, Gabrielle. Three years had passed since her death, but to me, it seemed like yesterday. Even now, she remained as vivid to me as the day she died, and sometimes I imagined opening my front door to find her sitting on the couch with Boo, watching one of her favorite movies, as if nothing grievous had ever happened. But it had. And my constant nightmares ensured I'd never forget.

A car turned up the street. I slid down in my seat just enough to see it pass, and then it turned and circled around before slowing to a snail's pace when it reached the curb in front of Parker's house. I took out my binoculars. It was dark outside, but the driver looked like a man. He gave Parker's place a long, hard stare and then put the car into park.

A couple minutes went by, and his car door opened. A heavyset man braced himself against the car and lifted his body out. He was dressed all in black and wore a long trench coat and a beanie cap on his head. He walked up to Parker's front door, looked over his shoulder, and then reached into his jacket, pulling out a small white envelope. He shoved it into the doorjamb and then shuffled back to his car. I put the binoculars on the seat and grabbed my camera, zooming in on the man's license plate. I snapped a photo. Moments later, he sped away.

My first instinct was to pilfer the envelope and look inside, but I wondered if the man might still be close by, watching. And since I didn't know Parker's whereabouts, I didn't want to get caught snooping around his place before I had the chance to talk to him.

If I wanted to take a peek at the contents of the envelope, I needed to act fast.

I dashed up to the door. The envelope had been left unsealed. Inside, I found a single index card with words written across the front in bold, black marker: *LEAVE HER ALONE OR ELSE.*

I stood there, staring at the card, assuming the warning note must have been referring to a woman who was living, and not one who was already dead. While I contemplated Parker being in a possible relationship with another woman, a car turned at the bottom of the street, heading in my direction. I crammed the card back inside the envelope and slid the envelope into the doorjamb. There was no time to get to my car unseen, so I did the next best thing. I assumed an army-crawl position and took cover behind a group of pine trees on the side of his yard. Seconds later, Parker's garage door opened and a car drove inside.

It was cold, and my clothes were getting soaked through, but I couldn't move—not yet. The garage door went down and a light illuminated from a room inside the house. Soon I had a clear view of Parker, who was pacing back and forth in front of an undraped window. As he walked, he talked on his cell phone. Every once in a while he stopped moving and laughed. Then he resumed pacing again. He was much skinnier than I'd imagined, *too* skinny for my taste, and the way his hand flicked when he talked exposed an air of confidence, like someone who reeked of money.

When the call ended, and he turned his back toward the window, I stood halfway up and sprinted for my car, making it part of the way across the street before the cold, hard ice I was running across became slippery, and I fell, my bum sliding bum along the pavement. Pain shot through me like needles piercing my skin. To bring myself to a stop, I pressed my palms into the ground in an attempt to gain traction, and then I pushed myself to a standing position and limped back to the safety of my car.

I had my hands on the steering wheel and my key in the ignition when Parker's front porch light turned on. Barefoot and dressed in a pair of striped flannel bottoms and a cotton shirt, he opened the door, and the envelope fell to the ground. He didn't seem to notice it at first. He bent down to retrieve the newspaper resting on his doormat, and that was when his eyes came to rest on the envelope. He picked it up, turning it over in his hand. Then he reached inside, pulling the index card out. He stared at the words written on the slip of paper.

A moment later, Parker reached back, flipping a switch on the wall in the foyer. The yard lit up on all sides. He walked to the edge of the porch, focusing his attention on the footsteps the man in black had left on the walkway leading up to the front door. He scratched his forehead and started to turn. It looked like he was headed back inside … until he spotted a second set of footprints in the yard. *My* footprints.

He stared down the road, and though the lamppost above my car wasn't lit, he made out the car sitting there and began walking in my direction.

Heart racing, I switched the ignition on and tore onto the street, my tires skidding along the ice as I raced down the hill.

We'd meet soon enough, but not today.

# CHAPTER 16

I returned home and found Nick at the house, wearing one of my aprons over his clothes.

"What do you think," he asked. "Does it suit me?"

I nodded and walked inside. I bent down to grab Boo off of the couch and winced.

"Are you hurt?" Nick asked.

I pulled my jeans down a few inches, revealing the source of my discontent. Most of the bruising was on my derriere and was taking on a nasty, purplish-blue effect.

Nick pointed the tongs in his hand at me. "You've got some explaining to do."

When the smell of Nick's cooking wafted past Boo, he wriggled around until I set him down, made his way to the kitchen, spun a few circles to show off, and then sat at Nick's feet, waiting to be rewarded for his efforts.

"You're a little mooch," Nick said. "It's a good thing you're cute."

Boo's eyes widened, and Nick squatted, offering him a small chunk of steak.

"There you go, you little moocher," Nick said.

"I should leave him with you more often," I said.

"I want to know about those bruises."

"On my way home tonight, I staked out Charlotte's ex-fiancé's place."

"And?"

"He wasn't home at first, so I thought I'd wait for a few minutes to see if he showed up. I wasn't planning on talking to him yet. I just wanted to see if he was in town. While I waited, the strangest thing happened. A guy pulled up and stuck an envelope in Parker's door. When he left, I walked over to see what it was all about."

Nick shook his head. "Couldn't leave it alone, could you?"

"Of course not," I said. "But Charlotte's ex came home before I made it back to my car."

"Let me guess. He saw you on his property and smacked your bum with a snow shovel."

We both laughed.

"I fell, on solid ice." I raised both palms. "This is what I get for all my hard work and effort."

"Ouch, you're missing some skin on those hands. Were you able to get out of there before he saw you?"

I shrugged. "I'm not sure. He knows someone was parked across the street from his house, but I don't think he could see my face through the tinted glass on my window, not at night."

"And the envelope … I'm guessing you opened it."

I nodded and told him what it said.

He raised a brow. "Huh. Weird just got weirder."

"I know."

"What about the guy who left the note? Did you get a good look at him?"

"It was dark, but I managed to snap a photo of his license plate."

"Good. Give it to me, and I'll run it."

"I'm perfectly capable," I said.

"Suit yourself, but you need to be careful, okay? Don't make me put a tracker on your car. You know I'll do it."

Given how possessive he was at times, I did. I could have had one on there now. It wouldn't surprise me.

We walked to the table, and Nick handed me a plate. One meal and a glass of wine later, I rested my head on the back of the sofa and took in the moment. I couldn't decide what I enjoyed more, the warmth of the fire or the peace that came from sitting in silence. I glanced at Nick, who didn't seem to share the sentiment. He was sitting beside me with a perplexed look on his face.

"You said we could talk about 'us' at dinner the other night, and we didn't," he said. "I know I haven't pushed the issue since, but you haven't brought it up again, either. You always put me off when I try to talk to you about anything that matters."

"I know. I'm aware I do it, but—"

"Whatever you need to say, Sloane, just say it. Get it out. At this point I don't believe putting it off any further will make a difference. You *know* how you feel."

Therein lay the problem. I cared too much about his feelings to just put the words out there so they could stab him in the heart like tiny verbal daggers. It didn't matter *what* I said. I had the uncanny ability of always saying the wrong thing.

Thinking a bit more wine might offer me an assist, I started to get up. He grabbed my waist, pulling me back down.

"Stop overthinking everything," he said, "and just talk to me."

"I don't overthink things. Not *everything*."

"Like hell. How are we supposed to have a decent relationship if we can't communicate with each other?"

"It's just … we see things so differently sometimes," I said.

He buried his head in his hands and talked through them. "So what…? We shouldn't try?"

I was only making things worse. He was frustrated with me, and I was even more frustrated with myself.

"You know what *you* want, Nick," I said. "But I'm not sure I do."

"What does that even mean? After all this time, how can you not know?"

"I think more about the here and now. You think about our lives together, our future."

"And you don't? I thought that's what we both wanted."

"I like what we have right now. I don't know why we have to change it. You have your place, and I have mine. We are together almost every night. Even with our careers, we see each other all the time. What about living together is so appealing to you?"

He sighed. "It's what I want."

"But it isn't what I want. Not yet."

I didn't know what else to say, so I said nothing.

Nick stood up and walked to the front door.

"You're leaving?" I asked.

Without turning around, he said, "Yep."

"This is why I don't like talking these things out. You don't agree with what I have to say and then you get angry. I need to be able to tell you how I feel without you blowing up on me."

He threw his jacket on and walked out the door, slamming it behind him. He'd shut me down, and there was no autopilot I could engage to fix it.

# CHAPTER 17

Parker's canary-yellow sports car weaved in and out of lanes, winding its way down Parley's Canyon to Salt Lake City. I stayed a fair distance behind, but without accelerating as he was, it was hard to keep up. I was wearing sunglasses and a brown bob-styled wig, which I'd tucked inside a paisley newsboy hat. Even if he hadn't seen me at his house the night before, I wasn't taking any chances.

We reached the bottom of the canyon, and the sky changed color, a defenseless victim of the inversion that had plagued the city for years. The once luminous skies were now a mutated, ashy shade of gray that reminded me of murky pond water.

Parker merged onto the interstate, making him harder to track. I sped up, just catching him as he took the exit on Six Hundred South and hit a red light. He sped through it, leaving me stuck behind two vehicles, and just like that, all my efforts were for nothing. I'd lost him.

For the next several minutes, I drove up and down the streets of the city but saw no sign of the car anywhere. According to Audrey, Parker had called her that morning, asking for the date and time of Charlotte's funeral. She suggested they meet up, and he said he couldn't. He was flying out in a few hours for work, but he would return to pay his respects.

I rounded Third South and caught a glimpse of a shiny, yellow diamond-in-the-rough parked in front of Rusty Nail, a new restaurant downtown. I parked my car and waited. The restaurant door opened some fifty minutes later, and Parker stepped out with his arm draped around a petite woman in a Bohemian-style cap with long, blond braided hair. She tilted her head back and laughed and then nuzzled into his shoulder. Pretty cozy for a man who should have been in mourning over the loss of a woman he'd tried so hard to get back.

Halfway across the street, Blondie stumbled a bit, which could have been because it was the restaurant's happy hour. He escorted her to a black Subaru. She reached out to open the car door, and he yanked her back, grabbing the door handle and opening it for her.

The perfect gentleman.

Blondie drove by, and I jotted down her license plate number. Parker returned to his car and revved the engine. I assumed he would head straight for the airport and was shocked when he turned his car in the opposite direction. His next stop was at a flower shop, where he emerged with a bouquet of lilies. He threw them in the passenger seat and drove to Lakewood Chateau, luxury condominiums designed like a hotel, with a doorman and a restaurant on the main level. The valet at the front took Parker's keys, and with flowers in hand, he headed inside.

I parked at the end of the street and went in after him. He entered the men's room in front of the restaurant, allowing me just enough time to stage an intervention. He exited the men's room a minute later and grabbed the bouquet of flowers he'd left with the woman at the front desk. I crossed by him, bumping him hard enough for the book and pen I was carrying to fall to the floor.

"I'm so sorry," I said. "I wasn't watching where I was going."

Parker bent down, grabbing the items I'd dropped.

Our eyes locked, and he grinned.

"No need to apologize," he said.

I held his gaze a bit longer and smiled.

"Well," I said, "thanks again."

I turned and started for the door.

"Wait just a minute," he said.

Hook, line, and sinker. It was too easy.

"At least give me your name before you leave."

"All right, then. It's Sloane."

He stuck out his free hand. "Good to meet you, Sloane. I'm Parker."

"Nice flowers," I said.

He scrutinized them for a moment, like he'd forgotten they were there.

"They're for my mother," he said. "It's her birthday tonight."

It sounded truthful enough, but I doubted it was.

"Well, Parker, nice to meet you," I said.

"You live around here?"

"Not too far."

"I haven't seen you before. If I had, I'm sure I would have remembered."

"It's a big city," I said.

He shook his head. "I meant, I haven't seen you here at Lakewood. Are you a resident?"

"Not yet. I'm in the market, though, so I thought I'd stop by today and check it out."

He nodded. "I see. It's a great place. You'll love it."

"I take it you live here?" I asked.

"Sometimes."

"And … other times?"

"I have a house in Park City, but I travel a lot for work. My family owns a private jet. I'm always heading off somewhere. It's a good life. I can't complain."

One would assume that line fascinated the ladies. A man with a house in Park City, a townhome on the side, a family jet, and a flashy sports car. Most women probably found him hard to resist. I wasn't most women.

Parker snuck a peek at his wristwatch. "My townhouse isn't like the others you've probably seen. I've made a lot of upgrades. You can take a look at it if you like."

"That's nice of you, but I don't want to—"

"It's no bother. I insist."

"How about we take a look at it right now?"

He grimaced. *Now* was no good. I wondered why.

"How about tomorrow?" he said.

He glanced at his watch again. There was somewhere he needed to be. If it wasn't the airport, where was it? And why had he lied to Audrey?

"Sure," I said. "Tomorrow sounds great."

"I'm number 312. Does eleven o'clock in the morning work for you?"

I nodded. "I'll see you tomorrow. Oh, and enjoy your mother's birthday party."

He picked a lily from the bouquet of flowers and handed it to me. "I look forward to tomorrow."

"Me too," I said.

More than he possibly knew.

# CHAPTER 18

Parker had been so swept up in our tête-à-tête he'd failed to notice the bug I'd planted in the pocket of his trousers when we collided. Now I just needed it to pay off. I walked back to my car and waited for the fun to begin.

To pass the time, I ran Blondie's license plate. Her real name was Zoey Kendrick. She lived in a suburb of Salt Lake City called Sugarhouse, which was about ten minutes away from where I was now. I jotted the address down for future reference.

Several hours and a cheeseburger and fries later, my listening device picked up the sound of someone knocking on Parker's door, followed by the click-clack of what I guessed were women's heels. I wondered if it was Zoey, heading over for round two of what they'd started earlier.

"I've missed you," Parker said.

There was some shuffling around and then what sounded like a kiss.

"For you," Parker said.

"They're beautiful," a woman's voice said.

Her voice was low and deep, and she had an accent.

"And you're even more beautiful. Come sit down. Tell me about what you've been doing since I last saw you. I want to know everything."

"Everything has been great. There's not much to tell."

"Are you happy to see me?" he asked.

"Of course."

I wasn't convinced. Something about the tone in her voice wasn't right. It was stiff and uncomfortable, like she was hesitant to be in the same room with him.

"I have something for you," Parker said.

"You didn't need to buy me anything. The flowers were enough."

"That's not what I meant."

There was silence for a short time, and then he said, "Take off your clothes."

The man wasted no time.

"I thought we were going out," the woman said.

"Our dinner reservations aren't for another hour. We have plenty of time, and I don't want to waste another minute of it."

"Parker, you said we could take things slow. This isn't my idea of pacing our relationship."

Their *relationship*?

"There's no need to play coy with me," he said. "I want you."

"Can't we talk for a while? I just got here."

"Come on, Daniela, please. Don't make me beg."

*Daniela?*

It seemed the proverbial poster boy of love lacked a faithful bone in his cheating, philandering body.

The bed creaked.

"Would you like to remove your clothes, or shall I do it for you?" he asked.

She didn't respond.

"Fine," he said. "If that's the way you want it."

There was movement on the bed and then a ripping sound.

"Stop it!" she said. "You're hurting me!"

"And what about *me*, Daniela? Have you considered what you're doing to me? Haven't I treated you nice? I bought you beautiful flowers, I made arrangements for an expensive dinner for the two of us, and this is how you show your appreciation—by refusing me? I don't think so."

"Stop it, Parker, please."

"*Stop it Parker. You're hurting me,*" he mocked. "You knew what to expect when you came here."

His voice had taken on an incensed tone, a far cry from the gentleman I'd met earlier. I started the car and slammed my foot down on the pedal. I didn't want to blow our meeting the next day, but no woman deserved this.

There was a crash and then a thud, and something hit the ground.

"Get back here!" he said.

A door slammed.

I pulled up in front of the building, and a dark-haired woman sprinted out. One look at her disheveled hair and bare feet, and I knew she was the woman I wanted. I pulled alongside her and put the window down.

"Daniela," I said, "get in."

"Why should I ... I don't know you. I need ... I need to call a taxi."

"I'm a friend. You can trust me. Please."

"I ... I don't know."

I grabbed the door handle and pushed the door open.

"Come on," I said. "Let me take you somewhere safe before he gets down here."

# CHAPTER 19

"Who are you?" Daniela asked. "And how do you know my name?"

I owed her an explanation. How much of one I wanted to give, I didn't know, but I had to say something.

"Where can I take you?" I asked.

"Cottonwood Heights."

"Are you okay? Did he hurt you?"

She shook her head.

"What about Parker?" I asked. "Did you hurt him?"

I hoped she had.

"His family jewels might be sore for a while," she said, "but I'm sure he'll survive. He always does. Wait—how did you know what happened at his place?"

"How do *you* know Parker?"

She glanced at me. "No more questions until you tell me who you are first."

"I'm a private investigator. I'm working a case he's involved in."

"Involved … how?"

"Have you known him long?"

"About a year."

"Were you two in a relationship?"

"If you mean in a romantic way, yes. We were."

"For how long?" I asked.

"About nine months. I broke it off recently. I never planned on seeing him again. He's very ... persuasive."

I wondered if Charlotte had found out about Parker's secret life. If she exposed it, or threatened to, it was possible she paid for it with her life.

"Why did you and Parker break up?" I asked.

She sighed and looked out my car window. "I don't want to talk about it."

"All right. Tell me when he hit you last."

Her eyes widened, giving me the confirmation I needed. Parker was abusive. Had he inflicted harm on Charlotte in the same way he had just done with Daniela?

"It's all right if you don't want to talk about it," I said. "I know we don't know each other. But it would really help if you were willing to share information about Parker with me."

She massaged her arm with her left hand, which jerked a tiny bit every time she touched it.

"Are you hurt?" I asked.

"I'm fine. I wanted to break it off for good this time, you know? That's why I went to see him. How could I be so stupid? I *know* who he is. I *know* what he's like. *Sono cosi stupido!*"

The phrase sounded Italian, but I had no idea what it meant.

"You loved him, didn't you?" I asked.

She hung her head and didn't respond.

"Do you know a woman named Charlotte Halliwell?" I asked. "Or Zoey Kendrick?"

She shrugged. "Should I?"

"From what I understand, they were both involved with Parker."

"That can't be true. How do you know this?"

"Parker was in a relationship with Charlotte. They planned to get married, but she called it off recently. I don't know much about Zoey, but I saw him with her earlier today."

Daniela made a fist and punched my leather seat, twice. "Bastard!"

"I believe he kept all of you in the dark, but I'm starting to wonder if Charlotte had found out he was seeing other women."

"Why don't you just ask her?"

"Because," I said, "she's dead."

Daniela gasped. "She's the woman who died at the ski resort, isn't she?"

I nodded.

"I'm sorry," she said.

"Me too. You could help me by telling me more about your relationship with him."

' I want to know something first."

"All right. What's your question?"

"How did you know I was going to meet Parker tonight? And how did you happen to drive up at the exact time I ran out, like you *knew* I was coming?"

In an attempt to lighten the mood, I said, "Would you believe me if I said I have impeccable timing?"

She wasn't amused. "Fine by me. You don't answer my questions, I don't answer yours."

It seemed we were at an impasse. If I wanted anything further, I needed to answer her questions. For the next several minutes I fed her rudimentary details about my interest in Parker Stanton and hoped she would keep quiet long enough for me to confront him first without blowing my cover.

When I finished, she said, "I don't even know what to think about everything you've just told me."

"At least now I hope you understand why I have so many questions."

"You want to know if I think Parker is capable of murder?"

"From everything I know of him so far, it seems he is. Anything you can tell me would help."

She leaned back in the seat. "At first, our relationship was different from anything I'd ever experienced before. I know it sounds cliché, but it was like a fairy tale. He left presents on my doorstep and notes on the windshield of my car, and we traveled together. Paris by day, London by night. Nothing was out of his reach. I guess some part of me questioned whether it was too good to be true, but I didn't want to believe it. No one in my life had ever treated me that way before."

"When did things change?" I asked.

"About halfway into the relationship, but by then, I'd fallen so hard for him, it was easy to make excuses about the things I didn't like and only focus on the things I did. Parker has a nasty temper. Anything can set him off."

"How did the abuse start?"

"At first he would just grab my arm or pin me down, but after a while, he became more aggressive."

"How so?"

"One day he shoved me, and I fell. He spent the next two days apologizing and said if I had it in me to forgive him, he promised to never lay a hand on me again."

"I'm guessing he didn't hold up to his end of the bargain," I said.

"For a couple of months, he did, and then not too long ago, we had dinner together. When we went back to his place, he blew up in a tirade. He hit me in the face, and it left marks. I backed up, trying to get away from him and tripped over the coffee table."

Daniela switched on the light on her side of the car, revealing a faded seven-inch bruise on the side of her abdomen.

"I thought he was the one, you know?" she said. "Charlotte wasn't the only woman he promised to make a future with. We planned our life together too. We'd talked about kids and everything."

Parker was starting to remind me of the gigolos I'd seen on television shows, the ones who'd been caught with multiple wives.

"Did you tell anyone what he did to you?" I asked.

She shook her head. "I wanted to, but I was embarrassed. I didn't want my family to find out what happened, so I left for a couple of weeks and visited a friend while I tried to sort it all out in my head."

"And when you returned, you decided to see him again?"

"I know what you think. How could I go back to that monster after what he did to me? All I can say is, he called me every day, and for a long time, I didn't answer … but the messages he left me were so sweet. Even with all we'd been through, I still loved him."

She pointed to the right. "Exit here and take a left at the stop sign."

I followed her instructions.

"You can pull over right here," she said.

I stopped the car. "Can I show you something before you go?"

"I guess so."

I pulled out my camera, searching it until I found the photo of the car I'd spotted in front of Parker's house in Park City.

"I stopped at Parker's last night, and he wasn't home. A man drove up and left a note in his door that said to 'leave *her* alone or else.' I wondered if you might know this guy? Maybe he left the note because of you?"

I handed her the camera and described what he looked like.

"This is the car he was driving," I said. "Do you know him?"

She gave me back the camera back and said, "No. I don't."

If she was telling the truth, why had I just detected fear in her voice?

She opened the car door, walked over to a wooden post, and punched in a code. A gate opened into a long road that wound around to a house so camouflaged with trees in front, it was hard to see.

"Nice place," I said.

"It's my brother's winter home. We only use it a few months out of the year during ski season."

His winter home?

I couldn't imagine what his summer home looked like.

"I'll walk from here," she said.

"Are you sure? I can drive you the rest of the way."

She shook her head. "It's best if you didn't. Thanks for the ride and the rescue. I'll never forget what you did for me tonight."

# CHAPTER 20

I was leaning against my headboard the next morning, staring at Boo who was snuggled up next to me. In a few hours, I'd meet with Parker. After experiencing his anger-fueled rage toward Daniela the night before, I wasn't sure it was a good idea to see him, but I wasn't about to cancel.

If Charlotte had been murdered, Parker was the number-one suspect on my radar, but learning about the other women he'd been seeing provided a strong secondary motive: jealousy. Daniela seemed nice enough, but was she? And then there was Zoey and the possibility of even more women I didn't know about yet.

My cell phone rang. It was Maddie. Before I could get a word in, she blurted, "Monkshood."

"Monkshood?" I asked. "What is it?"

"Our cause of death," Maddie said.

It sounded so unassuming.

"It's nasty stuff," she said. "The Greeks didn't call it the queen of poisons for nothing. It's ingested or absorbed into the system. There was enough in Charlotte's body to kill her a few times over."

It seemed Audrey was onto something.

"I can't believe it," I said.

"It's the perfect poison for a murder. It's possible someone gave it to her before she went skiing."

"Why do you say that?"

"Because it doesn't take long to work, and once it does, it has nasty side effects."

"Such as?"

"Paralysis of the facial muscles and the heart," she said. "It also dulls vision. At some point on the ski trail, she probably couldn't see where she was going. She could have been aware something was wrong, though, because although it's fatal, the recipient of the poison remains conscious right up to the end."

"What are the chances she came across the poison by accident, and it wasn't administered to her on purpose?"

"Highly unlikely. Whoever gave it to her probably thought he wouldn't get caught and assumed her death would be ruled an accident. He didn't take time to consider there might be a toxicology report if anyone thought otherwise."

"You said it doesn't take long to work. Are we talking minutes or hours?"

"I'd guess she died within a few hours of ingesting it. Maybe even less."

"What about her body? Other than the impact of the tree, were there any signs of foul play or any unexplained bruising?"

"Nope. Nothing."

Parker hadn't hit Charlotte. Not recently, at least.

"I'm meeting with Parker Stanton today, Charlotte's ex."

"Alone?"

"I'll be fine," I said. "Don't worry."

# CHAPTER 21

I took a deep breath in and knocked on door 312. There was no answer. I knocked again, harder this time. I wondered if what had happened the night before with Daniela had made him change his plans. Maybe the rejection had prompted him to run to one of his other many women I assumed he had on the side. I knocked one final time and said, "Hey Parker, it's me, Sloane, the woman you met yesterday in the lobby."

When that didn't work, I headed back toward the elevator. I'd almost made it when a door opened behind me, and I heard Parker say, "Sloane, hold up."

I turned my head and walked toward him.

He stared at me for a minute and then said, Oh, I'm sorry. I thought you were someone else."

"It's me." I gave it a minute to sink in. When it didn't, I added, "I … uhh … like to change things up, and the hat makes a big difference."

"Brunette bob-style hair yesterday, long hair today. Is it real this time?"

I nodded.

"I like it," he said. "You should wear it like this all the time."

*And you should mind your own business.*

I stepped into the dragon's lair and looked around.

"What do you think?" he asked.

"It's nice. It's very, umm, contemporary."

And cold and hollow, just like him.

"Would you like to look around?" he asked. "Or if you don't have anywhere to be, I can get you a drink. I have wine, beer, mixers."

I considered asking for a monkshood martini just to see how he'd react.

"I'm fine," I said. "Thanks ,though."

"Mind if I make myself a drink?"

"Go right ahead," I said.

He walked past me, limping. It was nice to see Daniela had made a lasting impact.

"What happened?" I asked. "Did you hurt yourself since I saw you last?"

He swished a hand through the air. "Oh, it's nothing. I tripped over a rug last night. I'll be fine in a couple of days. Just need to get some painkillers."

He mixed himself a frilly cocktail consisting of vodka and cranberry juice with fresh raspberries and even took the time to squeeze fresh lime into it before walking over and sitting down on the sofa. He tipped his head toward me, patting down the empty space next to him like I was a lap dog awaiting his command.

I bit my lip, mustered a smile, and denied him, choosing to sit on a chair instead. He laughed, seeming to enjoy the friendly game of cat-and-mouse he assumed we were playing.

"Tell me about yourself," he said. "Who are you, what are you, where are you?"

"I'm never good at talking about myself."

He crossed his legs and leaned toward me.

"All right, then," he said. "What should we talk about?"

"Do you know any real estate agents in the area?"

"Don't you have one already?"

"I did."

"I know every agent worth knowing around here. Who was it?"

"Charlotte Halliwell. Do you know her?"

He sat his drink down on the table and cleared his throat—twice.

"Charlotte Halliwell … huh."

I pushed harder. "Do you know her or don't you?"

"Yeah, she was an agent in Park City."

He spoke of her like she had been nothing more than a casual acquaintance.

It simply wouldn't do.

"How is it possible to be engaged to a person you're acting like you didn't really know?" I asked.

"Wait, what?"

"How did the *others* feel when they found out you had decided to marry someone else? Were they jealous, heartbroken, or did you keep the nuptials to yourself so you could continue seeing them as a side piece whenever you wanted?"

"The *others*?" he said. "What are you talking about?"

"You're other flings. The women you've been seeing on the side."

He stood up, staring at me, too stunned to speak.

"Just how many women do you have on the side, exactly?" I asked. "Three? Four? More?"

His brow was sweaty, and I hadn't even gone in for the kill yet.

"Who are you, really?" he asked. "And how do you know all of this?"

"Honestly, Mr. Stanton. If you want me to answer your questions, you should sit back down and consider answering some of mine."

I'd placed him in a position he wasn't sure how to get out of yet, a feat I imagined few women had been able to do before. I had become the cat, and he the mouse, and he didn't want to play anymore.

"Do you know how Charlotte died?" I asked.

He lowered himself back down on the sofa and leaned forward, resting his arms on his knees. "Yeah, some freak skiing accident."

"You're wrong, you know."

"What do you mean?"

"It wasn't an accident."

"What the hell are you playing at?"

His face conveyed genuine surprise, but it wasn't convincing enough to win the Oscar.

"Do you want to know how I believe she died?" I said. "I think she was murdered. What I need to know is, why?"

Shocked by my bold accusation, Parker spat some of his drink out. "You're just ... you're crazy!"

"I spoke to the medical examiner this morning. She believes Charlotte was poisoned. It makes sense if you think about it. Charlotte was an experienced skier. You know that. She was physically impaired on that ski run, and whoever poisoned her set it up so her death looked like an accident."

He shook his head. "I don't believe you. No way."

"Where were you on the day she died?" I asked.

"I know what you're implying, and you're wrong."

*Dead* wrong?

"Then answer the question," I said.

"We'd broken up. She wanted nothing to do with me, something I didn't accept, but still respected."

"Respected? What about the text messages you sent her on the day she died?"

"Look, I'm guessing you're not going to tell me who you really are, and I don't see a badge or a gun, so you're not a cop. I want you out of my house. Now."

"Just a few more questions first."

Parker slammed his glass down on the table and pointed at the door. "Get out!"

I stood. "One last question and then I'll go. Have you physically assaulted any women lately? Last night, perhaps?"

He launched off the sofa, shoving my body against the wall, pinning my neck with his fingers. I played the victim and allowed it. The rancid alcohol on his breath permeated the air. He kept me pinned for several seconds as he told me I shouldn't have come there. When he finished, I said nothing, further propelling an illusion of his dominance over me. He raised a hand to strike, a move I'd been waiting for. I snaked his arm with my free hand, yanking it toward me. This left him no choice but to open up his fingers. I jerked them back, watching as he yelped in pain. He released me, stumbling back, staring at the damage I'd done.

"You stupid bitch!" he yelled. "You broke my fingers!"

I raced to the door. He started after me, and I turned, pulling back my jacket just enough to reveal the gun holstered to my hip.

"That's far enough," I said. "Keep your hands off Daniela and any other women you've been seeing. If I hear you've smacked anyone else around, broken fingers will be the least of your worries."

# CHAPTER 22

Audrey and I arranged to meet at Charlotte's place. Maddie would follow a short time later, and the two of us would head to the police station to discuss our recent discovery. On the way to Charlotte's place, I tried calling Nick. He didn't answer, and I wasn't surprised. He was pouting, something he often did when things didn't go his way. I left a message.

The door to Charlotte's condo was unlocked when I arrived, and all the lights were on. I walked inside and said, "Hello? Audrey, are you here?"

A voice echoed from down the hall. "Yeah, I'm in Charlotte's room. Second door on the right."

I found Audrey sitting in the middle of Charlotte's bed, flipping through the worn pages of an old photo album. She traced her finger across a photograph of a much younger Charlotte, who was beaming with joy atop a purple bicycle with a yellow banana seat.

"Just reminiscing over all the good times we had together," she said.

I sat down next to her. "I think you were right about Charlotte's death being more than an accident."

Audrey closed the album and tucked it into a handbag. "What do you mean? What have you found out?"

She listened as I relayed the information Maddie had given me.

When I finished, she said, "I have to say, I'm kind of sad that I was right, but I'm also relieved. You know that feeling you get sometimes in your gut? I've had it all along. Ever since I sat at lunch on the day she died, waiting for her to join me. Maybe now that there's some evidence to warrant an investigation, everyone won't look at me like I'm a lunatic."

"The chief is a good man, Audrey. I believe he'll take us seriously now."

"It would be a good idea to arrest Parker before I get to him, because if I do, there's no telling what I might do."

"I know how you feel about his involvement in all of this, but I haven't proved it was Parker yet."

"He poisoned her. Isn't it obvious?"

"I confronted Parker a couple of hours ago, and he got aggressive with me. But I'm a lot better off than he is right now."

Audrey raised a brow. "What did you do?"

"Let's just say he won't get much use out of one of his hands for a while."

We both laughed.

"Good," she said. "Serves him right."

"You should know, he was seeing other women on the side. He had one of them at his condo downtown last night. He expected to have sex, and when she didn't consent, he lost it. She managed to get out of there, and I drove her home."

"What did she say? How long had she been seeing him?"

"About a year."

Audrey threw her hands in the air. "Unbelievable! I don't think anything you could tell me at this point will come as a surprise."

"Her name is Daniela. She said Parker hit her, and on more than one occasion."

"I knew he had a temper. I just want to wrap my hands around his scrawny little neck and squeeze."

"I need you to steer clear of him for now, Audrey. I mean it."

"You can't expect me to sit back and do nothing. He needs to pay for what he's done."

"And he will, but right now, I want to be sure we go about this the right way. Besides, we don't know what he's capable of. I'm not sure what would have happened at his place if I hadn't been able to stop him."

She rolled her eyes. "I'm *not* my sister. If I run into him, I can handle myself."

"I believe you, but let me see this through."

"Well, I got this far with your help, so I suppose I owe you that much."

"Did you ever notice any bruises on Charlotte?"

She shook her head. "She'd never said he hit her. Now that I think about it though, Charlotte dressed conservatively. If she *was* being abused, it's possible she could have hidden it from everyone. The medical examiner found no sign of abuse on her body. No bruises, scars, or anything other than the injuries she sustained in the accident."

Audrey glanced at a metal clock on the wall shaped like a cat and then reached for her bag. "I'm sorry, I need to run. Vicki boxed up some of Charlotte's personal effects at the office, and I said I'd head over and pick them up before she left for the day. But you can stay and look around for as long as you need to."

"And if you get the urge to confront Parker, call me first, okay?" I said.

"I can't guarantee I'll stay away from him forever, but for now, I will." She reached into her bag and pulled out a pack of cigarettes. "Just nail that son of a bitch before I change my mind."

# CHAPTER 23

Charlotte's condo presented itself as clean, but not meticulously so. A glass sat on the kitchen counter, half filled with water. It had a lipstick stain on the rim. I found another glass in the living room. It was empty. A pair of heeled shoes was on the floor in front of the sofa. One had tipped over on its side. Everywhere I looked I saw signs of life, and even though the apartment had become frozen in time, part of me felt like a trespasser waiting for Charlotte to walk through the door, wondering who I was and what I was doing there.

On a desk in a room she used as an office, I found a laptop. I opened it. It was password protected. I called Audrey, and she suggested I try the name "Charlie," a nickname her father had given Charlotte as a child. It didn't work. I tried a few others that didn't work either, and then Audrey said to try "Whiskers," the name of Charlotte's beloved cat that died a year before. That didn't work either, but Whiskers123 did.

I started with her internet files, and the six hundred unread emails junking up her inbox. Most were real estate related. I ran an inbox search on Parker, but it turned up nothing. On the days leading up to the murder, most of the emails in her sent folder contained responses to real estate questions and follow-ups with clients. I also found a monthly meeting she'd had with the real estate board and a couple of random emails to friends, but there was nothing out of the ordinary.

The top drawer of Charlotte's desk contained a file folder that had a stack of real estate transactions for the past year, all arranged in chronological order. I pulled the latch on the second drawer, but it wouldn't budge. I leaned over, looking at it more closely, and that's when I noticed a hole on the side of the desk about the size of a dime, just big enough for a tiny key to fit through.

I put myself in Charlotte's place. If I needed to hide a key, where would I hide it? I felt along the ridges of all the doors, but it wasn't there. I looked through drawers and jewelry boxes, pill containers and cups, all to no avail. Maybe the key wasn't in the condo at all. Maybe it was in Charlotte's car or in her office. On the other hand, if she accessed the drawer regularly, the key would need to be somewhere convenient.

I needed to look again.

I returned to the desk and opened the top drawer once more. I pulled everything out, and when I removed the box of thank-you cards, it rattled. I opened the box, but I didn't see a key. I dug through the cards and the envelopes, and sure enough, there it was at the bottom. I slipped it into the keyhole, and the drawer popped open. Inside the drawer I found two items: a notebook and a single file folder. I flipped the notebook open. There on the first page, scrawled on a sticky note were three names:

DANIELA LUCIANA
ZOEY KENDRICK
KRISTIN???

Charlotte *had* known about Parker's other women, but for how long?

I flipped a few more pages of the notebook and found a paperclip holding a business card and a few photos. The name on the card was *Marc Benjamin, PI*. I'd never heard of him.

I pulled the card off and saw a picture of Parker kissing Daniela. The next photo was of Zoey Kendrick and had been taken through a window of sheer curtains. From the waist up, she didn't have a stitch of clothing on. In the last photo, Parker was arm-in-arm with a brunette. I assumed it was Kristin.

I glanced at the time. Maddie would arrive at any moment to pick me up for our meeting with Chief Sheppard. I shut Charlotte's computer down, grabbed the contents of the drawer, and turned off all the lights inside the house.

As I turned to lock Charlotte's door, I smelled the faint aroma of cookies. One of Charlotte's neighbor's was baking—and making me hungry in the process. A wave of hot and then cold air brushed across my neck. I looked over my shoulder and caught a glimpse of a large object hurdling toward me. I ducked, but not in time. The object collided with the side of my head, my legs caved beneath me, and everything went black.

# CHAPTER 24

I woke in a field overflowing with white daisies. The sun blazed down, its warmth coalescing against my skin. I felt a sensation in my toe, like something was pricking it over and over again with a needle, and when I opened my eyes, a dainty, colorful butterfly was perched there.

I sat up and looked around. The place was unfamiliar to me, and yet I was at peace here, more so than I had ever been in my entire life. My body felt weightless, like a helium balloon floating into the sky. I didn't know where I was, and I didn't care. I closed my eyes and soaked it all in.

A voice called out to me, but I couldn't make it out. It was soft and melodious, like the entrancing rhythm of a blues song, and the more I listened, the more it became clear that I wasn't alone. Someone was calling my name.

I sat up and cupped a hand over my forehead, staring across the field at my sister. She was wearing a summery, white dress. I stood up, the stems of the flowers brushing along my feet as I ran toward her shouting, "Wait for me. I'm coming!"

But the more I ran, the farther away she became. I tried to run faster, but when I looked down, it was as if I were running in place.

I reached out to her. "Please, Gabrielle. I can't get to you. You have to come to me."

In a single moment, she was before me, her entire frame radiating with light. I looked in her eyes and felt a sense of calm and happiness. She reached out, and we embraced. It felt so nice to be near her, to feel her again.

"I am always with you," she whispered. "One day I'll come find you, and we can be together again."

I didn't understand. She was here in front of me. Why couldn't I be with her now?

She released me, raised her hand into the air, and waved at me before turning and walking through the trees.

Tears streamed down my face as I watched her go, yelling, "Gabrielle, wait! Don't go, please! Take me with you. I don't want to be here, not without you."

# CHAPTER 25

"Sloane, can you hear me?" a voice said.

I opened my eyes, but everything was a blur.

"Talk to me," a female voice said. "What happened?"

The woman's blond pigtails tickled my face. I tried swatting them out of the way, but my hand felt like a pile of bricks.

"Do I know you?" I asked.

"Do you *know* me? Sloane, come on. It's Maddie. Let me help you up."

"What happened?"

"I was just going to ask you the same thing."

I tried to speak, but nothing came out.

"We better get you to the hospital," she said.

"Hospital? What for?"

"Your head is bleeding, for starters."

She wrapped something around it and slung her arm around me. It felt like my legs were moving, but I wasn't sure. Maybe they were. "Where are we going?"

"To my car. Don't worry. It's right over there."

I looked *right over there* and didn't see anything except a big, blue blob with two bright circles on the front of it. The woman touched the side of the blob, and it opened.

"Watch your head," she said. "I'm guessing you don't know who did this to you?"

"Did what to me?"

"Whacked you over the head."

I sat down, and a minute later, we were moving.

"Do you have your phone on you?" she asked. "I need Nick's number."

"I … I don't know. Can you call her? I need to talk to her again. She needs to come back."

"Who do you need to talk to?" she asked. "Who needs to come back?"

"Gabrielle."

"Gabrielle's not alive anymore, sweetie. You're starting to scare me."

"I saw her, though," I said.

"Of all the times to open up about Gabrielle, you choose to do it now." She grabbed my hand and squeezed it tight. "It's going to be okay. Hang on for me, okay? Just a few more minutes and we'll be there."

She dug inside my jacket pocket, pulled something out, and said, "Hey, Nick? It's Maddie. Sloane is—"

There was a short pause.

"Listen," she said. "I'm not calling to talk about your relationship problems."

Another pause.

"Nick, for Pete's sake, shut up and listen. I went to meet Sloane at that dead chic's house, but when I got there, I found Sloane slumped on the ground in the doorway, bleeding. Looks like someone attacked her. She's sitting next to me now, going on and on about Gabrielle, and it's freaking me out."

I could hear a man's voice, but I couldn't make out what he was saying.

"To be honest with you," she said, "I don't know. She didn't know who I was when I found her. "

The man was now shouting.

"What I've told you is all I know right now," she said. "You want to know more? Meet me at the hospital. I'll be there in five."

She whispered something into the phone, too silent for me to hear, and then glanced over at me.

"Good, good," she said into the phone. "See you soon."

I tried to speak, but all I could get out was, "*mmmp mmy heaaad isss.*"

Going to explode.

That's what it felt like, at least.

# CHAPTER 26

I looked up to see Nick hovering over me. He was gripping my hand so tight I couldn't feel any sensation in my fingers.

"You feeling any better?" he asked.

I nodded. "Where's Maddie?"

"She went to find you some real food," he said. "Do you know what happened? Did you see who hit you?"

"I remember going to Charlotte's house," I said. "I messed around with her computer, but I didn't find anything, so I looked though the drawers and one needed a key."

"We can talk about all that later," he said. "I want to know what happened to your head."

"That part is still a little hazy."

"Try to remember. It's important."

"I walked outside and was locking Charlotte's front door, and I could feel someone's breath on the back of my neck."

"Did you see your attacker?"

"For a second. Not long enough or clear enough to make out who hit me. It all happened so fast. And then I opened my eyes, and Maddie was there."

"And that's all you remember?"

I nodded.

"Are you still mad at me?" I said. "Because I'm sorry about what I—"

The door opened, and an older man walked in, wearing a long white coat. "Ah, you're awake. Good, good. How are you feeling?"

I shrugged. "Fine, I guess."

"You gave your friends quite a scare. I'd like to ask you a few questions."

"Okay."

"What's your name?"

It seemed like a childish thing to ask, but I answered him anyway.

"And do you know where you are, Sloane?" he asked.

"A hospital, although I can't tell you which one. I'm guessing we're in Park City."

"Good, good. Who is the current president of the United States?"

"What if I tell you the name of my favorite president instead?"

He laughed. "I suppose that will do just fine."

"Did you know Lincoln was the first president to have a beard?"

He raised a brow. "Can't say I did. Your memory seems to be recovered. Still, I'd like to run a couple of tests before I let you go."

"Why? Is something wrong?"

"You sustained a concussion, one substantial enough to cause a temporary loss of memory."

"I feel fine now. What kind of tests?"

"The usual: strength, balance, coordination."

He grabbed my chart and went over it. "I've also ordered an MRI. It's nothing to worry about right now. I just want to make sure your brain isn't bruised or bleeding."

"I want to go home. When will that be possible?"

"Soon, I hope." The doctor patted me on the head. "I'll come back and check on you in a little while."

He walked out, and the chief walked in.

"How's the patient?" Sheppard asked.

"She'll live," Nick said.

"I'm glad you're here," I said. "We need to talk."

"No need. Madison filled me in already."

"There are a few things she doesn't know."

"Why didn't you come see me *before* going to the victim's house?" he asked.

"Aha! You called her 'the victim.' Does that mean you believe foul play is an option now?"

I may have been pressing my luck, but my head hurt, and I didn't care.

Nick piped up from the corner of the room. "I'm going to track Maddie down and give you two a chance to talk."

He grinned and exited the room.

And then there were two.

"Look, Sloane," the chief said, "you might think I don't give a rat's ass, but I do."

I adjusted my position in the bed and tried to sit up. "I know."

"You withheld information from me," he said.

"It wasn't my intention. After what happened between us the other day, I didn't want to come to you again unless I had substantially more to go on."

"Is that why you decided to confront Parker Stanton on your own?"

"How did you—?"

"Know?"

I nodded.

"He wants to press charges," he said. "Says you assaulted him in his home and broke some of his fingers."

I tried my hardest not to crack a smile.

"Well?" he said. "Did you break his fingers?"

"Not all of them."

He shook his head. "Aww hell, Sloane."

"Did he tell you he had me pinned up against the wall? I'll bet he left that juicy tidbit out. He abuses women. I caught him in the act last night, and I wouldn't be surprised if I found out he's the reason I'm in this place."

"We're working on a warrant, but given who he is and the pull his family has, it's not going to be easy. They'll fight it."

The chief rubbed his forehead, something he did whenever he needed to decide what to *do* about a problem. I didn't know if the problem was Parker, or if it was me or something else entirely.

"Can you give me the name of the girl he abused last night?" he asked.

I'd promised Daniela anonymity, and I wanted to keep my promise for as long as I could.

"I don't know very much about her," I said. "Let me get my thoughts together, and then we can go over everything I know."

He nodded and walked toward the door. "Come see me when you get out of here. And, Sloane, don't do anything else stupid."

# CHAPTER 27

I woke the next day to the sound of food sizzling in my kitchen. From the smell, I deduced it was of the swine variety. Boo was relaxed in his favorite position next to me: sprawled on his backside with his paws in the air like a dog's version of sun salutations.

Nick poked his head into the room. "You're awake. How's the head?"

"Good, I think. I'll survive."

He handed me a plate with enough meat on it to keep me full for a week.

"Wow," I said. "This is a lot of food."

He took the plate from me. "Let's try this again."

He handed it back, and this time I said, "This looks amazing. Thank you."

I grabbed the fork off the plate and dug in.

"The chief called earlier," he said. "He'd like you to stop in when you're feeling up to it."

I set the plate down and attempted to stand, but my legs had something else in mind.

"I need to talk to him today," I said.

"Whoa, hang on."

Nick took hold of my arm and helped me back to bed. "You're not going anywhere yet."

"Oh, come on, I just need a few minutes, and I'll be fine."

"Absolutely not. Now eat your food."

"You can be so stubborn sometimes."

He pointed at me and said, "I'm not half as stubborn as you."

I set the plate back on my lap. At the same time, Boo conducted a taste test, scarfing up a full slice of my bacon.

"Boo, no!" I said.

He ducked his head under the covers.

I looked at Nick. "Parker is dangerous. I'm worried about the other women. There's no telling what he might do."

"If he has any sense at all, he'll lie low a while."

"And if he doesn't? What if he hits someone else? What if he goes after Audrey? What if he disappears and we can't find him? What if—"

Nick held a hand out, stopping me. "Okay, okay. I get it. Why don't I call the chief and see if he can come to you instead of you going to him?"

"You want him to come *here*?"

"Take it or leave it. You're in no condition to go out right now. I don't care how tenacious you think you are. Today you're confined to this bed."

Boo poked his head out of the covers but avoided making eye contact with me. I patted him on the head, and he nuzzled up against my leg. He made his peace and returned to business as usual. If only life was that simple for everyone.

My cell phone rang. It was Vicki.

"Audrey told me what happened yesterday," she said. "I'm so sorry. How are you doing?"

"I'm fine."

"I'm glad your friend got there when she did. Talk about good timing. Is what Audrey said true? Is there really a chance someone murdered Charlotte?"

"It looks that way."

"Audrey is certain Parker's responsible for Charlotte's death."

"It's hard to say for sure."

There was an awkward pause that was just long enough for her to gear up for another round of questions.

"Thanks for calling, Vicki," I said. "But I'm still a bit out of it. I need to go."

"I understand. The reason I called is because Audrey mentioned you still haven't been able to talk to Charlotte's assistant, Bridget."

"No one can find her."

"She showed up here today," she said. "Yesterday, I'd heard she'd left town, but then I walked into the office, and there she was."

"Bridget's back at work?"

"Well, no, not exactly. She just came in to get some personal items she'd left behind."

"Did you talk to her?"

"I wasn't able to before she rushed out of here. One of the other gals in the office said she got a job somewhere else."

"Any idea where?"

"Sorry, no," she said.

"Do you know how I can get in touch with her?"

"She's still avoiding everyone's calls. When Jack found out she'd stopped by, he told his secretary to send her into his office, but Bridget rushed out of here before she got the chance. She's acting strange. At first, I thought it was because she's having a tough time with Charlotte's death. But now … I don't know. There's something else bugging her."

Nick walked in, saw the phone stuck to my ear, and shook his head. He grabbed my plate and walked back out.

"Sloane, you still there?" Vicki asked.

"Yeah, I wonder what's really going on with Bridget. I really would like the chance to talk to her."

"Let me ask around and see if I can find out where she's working now. Maybe that will help. She's a nice girl. We're all sad about what happened, but I guess I'd hoped Bridget and I could support each other through this. I thought we were friends. Guess I was wrong."

# CHAPTER 28

I did my best to spruce myself up, but I wasn't getting anywhere. I stood in front of the mirror, staring at myself. My large, brown doe eyes were usually one of my best features, but today there were dark circles beneath them. I looked about as good as I felt. Chief Sheppard was in the living room with Nick, and it seemed they were having a bit of fun at my expense.

"How's the patient today?" Sheppard asked.

"Feisty as ever," Nick said.

"Looks like the blow to the head didn't change much, then."

They both laughed.

"You better get in there before she comes tumbling out," Nick said.

I spared him from greeting me in bed and walked into the living room, doing my best to get my thoughts together. My hands quivered, which I attributed to the pain meds I was on. I didn't like it, and I didn't like not feeling like myself. As soon as the pain mellowed a little, the meds would find their way to the trash.

The chief saw me and smiled. "You look better."

He was lying, of course.

"Thanks," I said. "What's the latest?"

"My guys are digging up anything they can about Charlotte Halliwell in the weeks preceding her death."

"How do they know what to look for?" I said.

"I sent Coop to Wildwood this morning, and Calhoun here is headed to the real estate office where Miss Halliwell worked. And before you pipe up, I already know you went to both places. We're just doing some follow-up of our own."

The thought of Coop meddling in my case turned my stomach, something I was sure showed on my face.

"Now don't get up on that high horse of yours, Sloane," Sheppard said. "I know you disapprove. You and Coop need to bury the hatchet on this one and work together. I mean it. Whatever you think of him, he's good at what he does."

"He's the one with the problem," I said. "Not me."

"He wasn't always as hardheaded as he is now. There was a time when I considered him the life of the party."

I couldn't imagine it. "What changed?"

Sheppard stared at me, confused. "I thought you knew."

"Knew what?"

I looked at Nick, who acted like he knew more than I did but less than Sheppard.

"Coop had a daughter right around your age," Sheppard said, "and even though he disapproved about her decision to become a cop, she was also a fine officer."

"I overheard someone saying he had a daughter," I said. "I just assumed she didn't live here."

"She didn't. She lived in Chicago. She was shot in the head in the line of duty several years back—gang-related shooting. I bet you remind him a little of her the way you stick your neck out and take risks like you do. She was just as determined to do what needed to be done as you are. Heaven knows how proud he was of her, but after she died ... well ... you can understand how the death of a loved one changes a person."

More than I cared to admit.

It had never occurred to me that Coop acted like he did because of events that stemmed from his past, and though we had our differences, there was one thing we shared—the permanent scars of someone being taken too soon.

The chief sat down. "Let's talk about this Parker fellow."

"I want to make sure we're on the same page first," I said.

"Meaning?"

"If I tell you what I know, I want to be kept in the loop."

"I'll do what I can to include you in what we find, but you need to understand my position. I'm already sticking my neck out here."

"Just so I understand, you're agreeing to keep me updated on any breaks in the case and any new information you come across, right?"

"Let's face it," Sheppard said. "We both know Calhoun does that already. And there's no need to cover for him with some bullshit story about how the two of you keep work and personal stuff separate. I have a wife. I know better."

I exchanged glances with Nick, who was acting aloof, maybe because there was some truth to what the chief said, but not as much truth as the chief assumed.

"I also want to be involved in the interrogations," I said.

"You know I can't put you in the room."

"You can give me access to the recordings."

"I'm not sure that's such a good idea."

"No one has to know except the three of us. If it weren't for me, you wouldn't even be pursuing this case."

"All right. I'll think it over," he said. "Can we get on with it?"

I gave him a brief overview of Parker's womanizing ways, talked about Daniela's ordeal without using her name, and detailed my visit with Parker on the day I was attacked.

When I finished, he said, "So he likes the ladies. It doesn't make him a killer."

"Not yet, but it gives him motive. Plus, he's abusive. Maybe he abused Charlotte, and she threatened to go public. He wouldn't want to tarnish his family's perfect image. Maybe he couldn't handle the breakup, or maybe she found out about the other women and …"

The other women!

I'd almost forgotten about the photographs I'd found in Charlotte's drawer.

Sheppard leaned forward. "You were saying?"

Until he held up his end of the bargain, I decided it wouldn't be a bad thing to keep a few minor details to myself.

"I don't believe it was a coincidence that on the same day I confronted Parker, I was attacked at Charlotte's place," I said. "I think you should turn up the pressure. We need to know if Parker had anything to do with Charlotte's death or if we need to go in another direction."

"Maybe, I don't know."

He didn't know?

"Bring him in," I said. "See what he has to say for himself. Ask him where he was on the day of Charlotte's murder. If you need a reason to pick him up, I'll press charges of my own."

Sheppard stood. "Well, kiddo, I'll let you get some rest. Let's see where we're at later on. You two have a good day."

# CHAPTER 29

My laptop sat on a chair in my room next to my grandfather's old T.H. Robsjohn-Gibbings desk. Sometimes I imagined him sitting there putting the finishing touches on a piece of jewelry he'd made out of variegated rocks he found on one of his treks through the desert. The paramour of my collection included a necklace he'd made for me out of tiger's eye, but it wasn't the bold yellowish-brown hue or even the look of the necklace that attracted me. I liked the way it sounded: *tiger's eye*. It was powerful, and I felt powerful when I wore it. As a child I had no idea how much the pieces would mean to me when he was no longer around to make them.

One day had come and gone, and I was still mentally out of it. Even standing was a chore, so I decided to take an easier road and dug into my sheets with both hands, inching my way toward the edge of the bed. Five heave-hos later and I grabbed my laptop off the chair and performed a search of private investigators in the state of Utah by the name of Marc Benjamin. My efforts yielded one match. I dialed the number.

"This is Marc," he answered.

"My name is Sloane Monroe," I said. "I wondered if you could help me."

"What can I do you for?"

"I'd rather discuss it in person, if you don't mind. Can we meet?"

"Sure can. How about tomorrow afternoon?"

"I need to speak with you today, if that's possible."

There was a short pause. "I have plans in a couple of hours, but if you could get here soon, I'll make it work."

"Great, see you in a bit."

I wrestled stripping off what I had been wearing and managed to pull a hoodie over my head and slip on a pair of yoga pants. I gazed into the mirror. In the appearance department, I was in an hour of need. I pulled my hair into a loose bun and headed for the door.

A cabbie dressed in all black hopped out and opened my door. He had a clean-shaven, oversized head and a moustache that trailed down on both sides into a goatee. He stared at the bandage on my head but said nothing.

"Where to, lady?" he asked.

"University Avenue, across from the Riverdale Shopping Plaza."

He nodded, and away we went, winding past the double cataract waterfalls at Bridal Veil Falls, which usually had a magnificent display of cascading water showering down into the Provo River. But we were in the dead of winter, and the water had turned to spiky tentacles of ice.

The office of Marc Benjamin, PI, looked a lot more like a renovated old house than a professional establishment, but after checking the address once more, I confirmed I was in the right place.

I walked inside and became overwhelmed by the powerful smell of fresh paint. The sound of footsteps approached from behind.

"Like it?" the man asked. "Painted the walls yesterday. Color is called Navajo White."

He said Navajo like *nav-ee-hoe*, and it looked like plain, ordinary white to me.

"Are you Sloane?" he asked.

I nodded.

He wiped his hand on his oil-stained jeans and offered it to me. I wasn't inclined to take it, but for the sake of his gesture and because he agreed to meet me on short notice, I did.

"Sorry about the dirt and grime," he said. "I just finished loading some bales of hay."

"You *are* Marc Benjamin, right?"

He tipped his cowboy hat in my direction. "At your service, ma'am."

We walked toward a desk in the corner of the room and sat down.

"What can I do you for?" he asked.

"Have you been in the business long?"

"Not really. This is just something I do on the side for fun."

I suspected as much.

He stared at the main attraction on my head. "What happened, if you don't mind me askin'?"

"Bullfight," I said. "The bull won, and now I have to wear this hideous thing for a few days."

He slapped a hand down on the desk and grinned. "Well now, you sure are funny."

"I wondered if you could give me some information about one of your clients."

"Probably not. It's important to respect their privacy and all."

"The client is Charlotte Halliwell. You know she died, right?"

The revelation startled him.

"It's all over the news," I said. "You didn't know?"

"I've been in Texas visiting one of my kids. I only got in a couple of hours ago. Haven't had much time to catch up with all the local goings-on yet. When did it happen?"

"A week or so ago."

"Charlotte sold my dad some horse property over in Heber Valley last year. That's how we met and became friends. She planned to buy one of our mares this year. A few months back, she came out to the ranch. She said she rode as a kid and wanted to get back to the simple things in life."

"I hate to tell you this," I said, "but I'm investigating her death, and I believe she was murdered."

He sighed. "You don't say? How'd she die?"

I told him.

"Who in their right mind would want to hurt such a nice person?" he asked.

"I was hoping you could tell me. I need to know why she hired you."

He pulled his hat off, smoothed a hand over his hair, and stuck it back on again.

"I'm a private investigator myself," I said, "so I understand your loyalty to her, even in death. But in our business, it helps when we can pool our information together. If someone murdered her, we both want the same thing, right?"

It wasn't the best pep talk I had ever given. It wasn't the worst either.

"Truth be told, the kind of research I usually do is of the genealogical kind. I only took this on as a favor to Charlotte because she was paranoid that if she went to someone else Parker would find out."

He walked over to a plastic bin in the corner of the room and dug through some of the files. "Charlotte came to me about three months ago. She thought her fiancé had another lady friend in his life."

He pulled out the same photos that I had come across at Charlotte's house.

"There were others, all right," he said. "The man went after every woman he could get his hands on, from the looks of it."

"How did Charlotte react when you gave her the news?"

"She thanked me for the information, but she seemed ambivalent. I got the feeling she'd suspected it for some time and had come to terms with the truth beforehand."

"When you were keeping an eye on Parker, did you see him abuse any of the other women he was seeing?"

He shook his head. "I only tailed him for two days. Once I told Charlotte what I'd found, she didn't want me to take it any further."

"Did you speak to her again?"

He nodded. "A few weeks later."

"What about?" I asked.

"She told me she'd canceled the wedding and was feeling a lot more like herself than she had in a long time. She said it was time to unclutter all the clutter in it."

I wondered if Parker had been the only clutter she was referring to.

"Did Charlotte say how Parker reacted to the news?"

"He denied seeing other women, but then she showed him the photos I'd taken."

"Can I get a copy of the file you have on her?"

He thought about it for a minute. "I suppose. I can scan the pages if you'd like."

I liked.

He went into another room. A few minutes later, he returned and handed me a manila envelope. "I'll admit, when she said she'd dumped that guy, I'd planned on asking her on a date even though I'm a good seven years older. But I figured she probably needed a little time first, you know, to heal and everything. Now I wished I had and that I would have been there for her. Maybe it wouldn't have made much of a difference, but then again, maybe she'd still be alive if I had. If I can do anything else, just holler."

I thanked him for the information, and he smiled, tipping his hat toward me. "You have a good day, now."

## CHAPTER 30

Nick wasn't happy when I arrived back home.
"I thought we agreed you needed to stay home and rest," he said.
"I'm sorry," I said. "I needed to visit with someone. It was important."
"I called your cell several times," he said. "You could have answered."
Boo bolted around the corner with his tongue out, giving me a much more exciting welcome.
"I lost phone service in the canyon," I said. "I don't have a missed call from you."
He eyed me suspiciously until I showed him the call log.
"All right, fine," he said. "You need rest. You're in no condition to be out running around. How are you supposed to protect yourself when you're not one-hundred-percent yet?"
"We don't *know* anyone is after me personally. I'm not dead. Maybe whoever clocked me in the head was only after something in Charlotte's house."
I changed into a tank top and flannel bottoms. When I walked back into the kitchen, Nick reached for a paper bag on the counter. He pulled out a container of sweet and sour chicken and dangled it in front of my face.

"I will give you this entire box of chicken and even throw in a side of wontons if you agree not to run off without telling me first," he said.

The wontons looked good enough to donate a body organ for them.

"Do we have a deal?" he asked.

I nodded and grabbed a couple of plates.

"Where were you this afternoon?" he asked.

"I went to see the private investigator Charlotte hired."

"And?"

"I managed to get a little information from him, but not much. The guy was nice, and I could tell he wanted to help, but he looked more like a farmhand than a detective."

"Neither of us got anywhere, then, from the looks of it," he said.

"Where did you go today?"

"I stopped at the real estate office and spoke to Vicki."

"How did that go?"

"Probably about the same as when you went to see her. She answered our questions, but we didn't learn anything useful until we were on our way out."

"What happened then?"

"One of the other agents in the office said he witnessed Parker losing his temper last summer after a work-related dinner attended by everyone in the office and their spouses."

"He lost his temper with Charlotte?"

Nick shook his head. "Not with Charlotte. With her assistant, Bridget Peters."

# CHAPTER 31

The bitter chill of winter nipped at my face as I raced to the warm sanctuary of Nick's car. Fog hung in the air like a wedding veil, and the roads were saturated with snow. Snowplow workers pushed it off the streets into steep, ten-foot mounds that resembled heaps of dirty glaciers. The elements could do their worst. With Parker on the hook, nothing would stop me from being there when they questioned him.

Coop grinned at me when we entered the station, which wasn't a good sign.

"You're too late," he said. "You missed the dog-and-pony show."

He wasn't about to break my spirit, not today.

"I haven't missed anything," I said. "I'm here to view the recording."

"I like the new headdress," he said. "You should be more careful."

The chief glared at Coop and then summoned me to his office. I walked in and sat down. "How did the interview with Parker go?"

"He lawyered up, so we couldn't get much out of him," he said.

"Figures. Who questioned him?"

"Coop."

That figured as well.

"Parker denied any involvement in what happened to Charlotte Halliwell, of course," the chief said. "Claims he was in New York at the time. He seemed broken-up about her death, but I wasn't convinced."

"Can anyone back up his alibi?"

"He says a woman can. A female friend of his."

Of course. The real question was—which one?

"Who's the woman?" I asked.

"Kristin Tanner."

My mystery woman had a last name after all.

"Have you tracked this *friend* down?" I asked.

"She lives in New York, but she's flying in tomorrow for the weekend. We'll question her then."

"Let me guess … she's staying with Parker."

He nodded.

"How hospitable of him," I said. "What did he have to say about the abuse?"

"Denied it. And since no one has come forward, there's not much I can do."

"What about me? I came forward. That jerk had me in a chokehold."

"And he's the one with the broken fingers," he said. "It's his word against yours."

"And you don't believe me?"

"I didn't say that."

"You might as well have."

"It's not a question of whether I believe you. You know I do. You're aware of how the system works. If I'm going to arrest the guy, I want the evidence to be solid enough to keep him locked up."

"So, for now we let him walk, free to roam the city, striking women at his leisure?"

"You're being ridiculous," he said. "He's well aware we're keeping tabs on him."

For now.

What happened when the legal eye in the sky was no longer watching?

"Parker Stanton should be in a jail cell," I said. "And I'll bet Daddy Stanton did what he needed to do so his precious son could stroll right out of here."

I stood up and opened the office door, ready to walk out. The chief leaned over the desk and grunted, "Shut the door and sit back down."

I didn't want to shut the door. I wanted to slam it. Ever since the accident, I hadn't felt like myself. I didn't know what to blame it on: the prescription drugs, the lack of a decent night's sleep, or maybe it was the guilt I harbored over not proving who'd killed Charlotte yet.

I faced the chief but remained at the door.

"I put a tail on Parker," the chief said. "I'm not letting him go for nothing. If there's something he's hiding about Charlotte's murder, I can assure you, I won't rest until I figure out what it is."

# CHAPTER 32

The recording began with the usual rigmarole. Coop dispensed the formalities by asking the customary questions to Parker, whose lawyer was in the room with him. Parker appeared calm and collected in the uncomfortable metal chair, which had been placed with much consideration in the corner of a stark, white room. At the beginning, Parker sat up straight like a schoolboy eager to impress the teacher. He wore a fitted black suit, a drab tie, and had one leg crossed over the other, portraying a casual, exemplary image.

When Parker spoke, his words were articulated with perfect finesse: *yes sir, no sir, thank you officer*. He even cracked a joke in an attempt to get Coop to smile. Coop was many things, but a dummy wasn't one of them.

The formalities began, and Parker smiled, satisfied he'd made a good first impression. But I knew Coop, and he hadn't. The tables were about to turn. I was sure of it.

"Tell me about your relationship with Charlotte Halliwell," Coop said.

"There's not much to say," Parker said. "We dated for a while. Things got serious, and we even talked about getting married later this year, but it didn't work out. I broke it off."

Lies.

"When did the relationship end?"

Parker shrugged. "Maybe three, four months ago, I guess."

"Why did you break off the engagement?" Coop asked.

"I wasn't ready for it."

"You weren't ready for *what*—marriage?"

Parker nodded.

"Why not?" Coop asked.

"Charlotte was clingy, and I need my space. So I decided it wasn't worth it. You're a man. You understand what it's like to feel suffocated, right?"

Interesting choice of words.

"And Charlotte, how did she take it when you broke things off?" Coop asked.

"She begged me to get back together with her."

More lies.

"And did you?"

"No sir. I had already moved on with someone else."

Clearly the understatement of the year.

Coop switched gears. "Let's talk about the day she died. Where were you?"

"I was in New York, working."

"Were you alone that day or with anyone who can back up your story?"

"I was with a friend."

"What kind of *friend*?"

"Does it matter?"

Coop tipped his head like he was giving it some thought. "Dunno. Might."

"She's a good friend. Satisfied?"

"And can this—"

"Kristin Tanner."

"Can Kristin Tanner back up your story?" Coop asked.

"She flies in this weekend. You can ask her yourself."

"When did you see her last?"

"Kristin?"

"Charlotte."

Parker stared at his fingers like he was trying to count it out. "Not for a couple months, at least."

"Interesting," Coop said.

Parker attempted to lean back in his chair, but the metal on the legs skidded around on the floor, causing the chair to slide while he continued to squirm in his seat. "Why is it interesting?"

Coop leaned forward, sticking a finger about an inch from Parker's face.

"A valet at Wildwood puts *you* outside Miss Halliwell's car about three weeks ago," Coop said.

Parker seemed startled by the accusation. And he wasn't the only one.

"I'll ask you again," Coop said. "When was the last time you saw her?"

"I told you, a couple of months ago. The valet must have me confused with someone else."

Coop turned up one corner of his mouth. Parker didn't notice, but I did. Coop had him right where he wanted.

"You're sure you want to stick with that story?" Coop asked.

Parker's hotshot lawyer, who hadn't said a word up to now, decided it was time to earn his keep. "I'm not sure what you're playing at, Mr. Cooper, but I won't tolerate you harassing my client."

"It's *Detective* Cooper, and I asked a simple question."

"And I answered it," Parker said.

Coop recoiled back in his chair. From the look on his face, his line of questioning was far from over.

"Let me lay it out for you, son," Coop said. "The witness said you confronted Miss Halliwell at her vehicle, and when she tried to open her car door, you stopped her."

Parker scoffed. "Ridiculous. Never happened."

"Oh, I'm not done. You also physically held her down, pinning her against the car."

"This is outrageous!" the lawyer said. "He's already addressed the question. Why do you keep drumming on, badgering him about it? It *wasn't* him, and he *wasn't* there."

"You were there, son," Coop said. "You can lie about it if you like, but you know it, and I know it."

Parker loosened his tie and adjusted his collar, which appeared a bit damp. He uncrossed his legs and leaned back. "I came in voluntarily. If all you're going to do is falsely accuse me of something I didn't do, I'm done answering questions."

Coop glared at Parker. Parker glared back. The lawyer looked at his legal pad and pushed the top of his pen up and down. It made a snapping noise.

Parker dabbed the corners of his eyes with a finger, like he was drying the non-existent moisture off of them. "I want you to find the barbarian who ended Charlotte's life. I really do. Despite what you people think, or what you'd like to accuse me of, I loved her. I wanted a life with her. I wanted children. We may have called off the wedding, but I still thought we had a future. And now I've been robbed. She's been taken from me."

He'd done it—turned everything around and made himself the victim.

Coop considered Parker's sentiments and then said, "Would you like to help me, Mr. Stanton? Would you *really* like to help me?"

"I'm here, aren't I?"

"Good. Cut the bullshit and tell me the truth."

Parker leapt out of his chair and grabbed his lawyer's arm, jerking him out of his seat. In unison, they headed for the door.

"Enjoy the rest of your day, Detective," Parker said.

Coop waited until Parker reached for the knob before he spoke. "Oh, I will. Would you like to know how I'm going to spend it?"

"What interest is it of mine?"

"Did you know Wildwood has twenty-four-hour surveillance cameras set up in almost every location of the resort? Five in the parking area alone. I'm expecting the footage to be delivered shortly."

Parker loosened the death grip he had on the knob and turned to his lawyer. They exchanged glances. The lawyer sighed, closed the door, and whispered into Parker's ear.

"Let's go over this one more time," Coop said. "You went to Wildwood on the day in question and assaulted Miss Halliwell at her car."

Parker looked at his lawyer, who shook his head, prompting Parker *not* to say another word.

"I don't care what it looks like or what you'll see on those tapes," Parker said. "We engaged in a civilized conversation between two people. I'll admit I got a little angry with her. It's not a big deal. Couples fight all the time."

"Don't say another word," the lawyer said.

"You got angry," Coop said. "Proves you have a temper."

Parker laughed. "Doesn't everyone?"

"Not everyone hits women," Coop said. "I don't."

Parker's lawyer applied a fair amount of pressure to his arm. "I must advise you not to say another word, Parker. We're done here."

Parker nodded, reached for the knob again, and then winced. He stared at his hand like he was having a flashback of our confrontation.

"By the way," Coop said, looking at Parker's bandaged hand, "how did it *feel* to get beaten up by a girl? Sloane's a feisty little fireball when she wants to be. Am I right? Still … she's a woman, and you're a … well … a man. Aren't you?"

Parker returned the comment with an icy stare, but his lawyer shoved him out the door before he had the chance to say anything further.

The interrogation was over.

# CHAPTER 33

"I wanted to ask you a few more questions," I said.

"Sure, come on in," Vicki said.

Today she was wearing a black skirt with thin white pinstripes and a button-up that was tucked in. After we greeted each another, one of the buttons on her shirt popped off. Aware of the wardrobe malfunction, she crossed her arms in front of her chest as she talked to me.

"Did Charlotte keep copies of her files here at the office?" I asked.

"We have different types of files. Which ones are you referring to?"

"Both. Her client files and real estate transactions."

Vicki motioned to the pair of file cabinets between the two desks. "We keep all client files for the current year in the cabinets. But nothing's in there now."

"Why not?"

"Charlotte bought new color-coded file folders about a month ago and took them home to switch them over. The old ones were falling apart."

I thought back to the night I was at her place. The folders I saw must have been the old ones. They weren't color-coded.

"What about real estate transactions?" I asked. "Where are those kept?"

"All sale documents are kept downstairs with the office manager. Her name is Wanda. I can call down and see what we can find for you, if you like."

She picked up the phone.

"That's okay," I said. "I'll talk to her on my way out."

Vicki nodded and placed the phone back on the receiver.

I pointed to Charlotte's empty desk. "What about Charlotte's office computer? Last time I met with you, it was on her desk. It's gone now."

"One of the other agents has it. It belonged to the agency, not Charlotte. She never used it much anyway. She liked to keep things on her laptop."

"Did she have problems with any of her clients? A disgruntled seller, perhaps, or a buyer unhappy with the purchase they'd made?"

"It does happen in our business from time to time, but no one comes to mind. Let me think about it. I thought you were focusing on Parker Stanton?"

"We are," I said, "but I wouldn't be doing my job if I didn't explore all of the angles in this case."

"Good idea. I've thought about it, and I'm still not sure he would hurt Charlotte—not to the point of killing her, anyway."

"Did Charlotte ever mention Parker's *other* women to you?"

Vicki looked surprised. "I'm not sure what you mean."

"I'll take that as a no," I said.

"Are you being serious? Were there other women?"

I nodded. "A few. Maybe more. If Parker isn't responsible for what happened to Charlotte, it's a possibility one of his lovers might be."

"Did Charlotte know he was seeing other women?"

"Looks like it. She hired a private detective to keep tabs on him."

"Wow. Well, she never said anything to me. Charlotte kept private things to herself, though. We were good friends, but even so, she wasn't the type of person to share the most personal aspects of her life very often."

I stood. "Thanks for seeing me again. I appreciate it."

She nodded. "No problem. Let me know if there's anything more I can do to help."

## CHAPTER 34

I reached the bottom of the stairs and knocked on Wanda's office door. She called me in, and I went inside, finding Wanda on the phone, sitting at her desk. She had short, poodle-looking hair and wore a knitted sweater with a mallard duck on the front. She stared up at me like I had intruded on her personal space and then held a finger up to ensure my silence while she continued her phone conversation. I waited in silence along with an array of fifty or so troll dolls lined up on a wall shelf behind her.

After a three-minute wait, Wanda ended the call, shuffled some paperwork around, and then glanced in my direction. "Yes? What can I do for you?"

"I'm looking into the death of Charlotte Halliwell, and I hoped I could get a copy of her files."

"And you are a what … cop? A reporter? Who are you?"

I took a business card out of my wallet and presented it to her. She opened the middle drawer of her desk, scattered some items around, and pulled out a pair of reading glasses. She put them on and scrutinized the card like she didn't believe it was authentic.

"Well, Sloane Monroe, PI," she said, "can I see the warrant?"

"It doesn't work that way."

"It doesn't work *what* way?"

"Technically, I'm not with the police. Charlotte's sister hired me to investigate the circumstances around her sister's death, and I hoped you could—"

"Well, *technically*, no warrant, no files. I know my rights."

My intermittent charm had no impact on her. I tried a more direct approach.

"I don't need to take them out of the office. Can I just glance at them?"

She flicked the business card I'd given her into the trash. "Sure. You bring a warrant, you get the files."

"I can get the chief of police on the phone. I'm sure he would give you the go-ahead."

"Then do it," she said.

I thought about it for a moment, unsure of whether he'd actually support me if I called, and decided it wasn't worth the risk. Not yet.

"I'm heading into the police station," I said. "I'll ask him and get back to you."

She shrugged. "Whatever. Makes no difference to me."

# CHAPTER 35

The iron gates in front of Daniela's brother's mansion in the trees were closed when I drove up. I stopped in front of them and pressed the buzzer.

"Yes?" a male voice said on the other end. "What can I do for you?"

"Can I speak with Daniela?" I asked.

"And you are?"

"A friend."

"Do you have an appointment?"

Did I have an appointment?

"I … umm … didn't know I needed one," I said.

"Is she expecting you?"

"No. Is she here?"

"Maybe. Your name?"

"Sloane."

"Sloane what?"

"Monroe."

I thought about throwing my middle name in for kicks, but decided I'd better not press my luck.

There was movement outside the car window. I stuck my head out and looked up, seeing a video camera disguised in the branches of the tree. It made some adjustments and then lined me up in its sights.

"Daniela is not here right now," the voice said.

"Can you tell me when you expect her?"

"No, I cannot."

"Can I leave a message?"

"You can. What do you wish to say?"

"Can you ask her to give me a call?" I asked.

"Does she have your number?"

"She does. I'll leave it again, though."

I gave him my number and waited.

"Thank you," the voice said. "I'll be sure to pass it along. Goodbye, Miss Monroe."

The camera stayed with me while I backed out of the drive and turned around.

*Who were these people?*

On my way down the road, I spotted a slender jogger. She ran past me, but didn't glance in my direction. Her thick, black glasses shielded most of her face, but the hair was unmistakable. I did a U-turn.

"Daniela," I said. "Hey."

Headphone chords dangled from her ears, and she didn't hear me at first. I moved a bit closer. She looked at me, and I waved.

She removed her headphones, squinted, and then crossed the road.

"Oh, it's you," she said. "What are you doing here?"

"I need to talk to you about Parker," I said.

"It's like I told you the other day, we're over. There's nothing left to say."

"I know. I just wanted to warn you."

She jogged in place as she continued talking. "Why?"

"Charlotte Halliwell was poisoned. Her death wasn't an accident."

Daniela brushed a fallen piece of hair out of her face. "Oh my gosh. I'm sorry."

"At the moment, Parker is the number-one suspect. I thought you should know in case he tries to contact you."

She didn't seem the least bit concerned. "Did you go to the cops?"

"I'm helping them out with the investigation," I said.

"You promised you'd leave me out of it. I don't want the cops involved with what happened the other night."

"I know. I haven't revealed your identity. Look, we both know Parker has a lot of pent-up anger. You need to be careful."

Daniela tossed her head back and laughed.

"Yeah, well, don't worry about me. He'll stay away if he knows what's good for him. If he comes anywhere near me again, my brother will …"

She stopped midsentence and stood there.

"Your brother will what? Who is your brother, anyway?"

"I gotta go," she said. "Thanks for the warning."

## CHAPTER 36

"Home yet?" Nick asked.

It was five o'clock in the evening, the absolute worst time to leave Salt Lake City.

"Not even close," I said.

"Guess what I've got?"

"A way to make all of these cars disappear?"

"I have something even better," he said. "I have the address of the guy Charlotte's assistant is dating, and I'm on my way there now. Care to join me?"

"Do you need to ask?"

"Meet me off the Summit Park exit, and we'll ride over together."

Nestled along the hillside amongst a myriad of pine trees, Summit Park was the first stop before locals and visitors descended into Park City. From the highway, a mix of old and new homes dotted the landscape. A week earlier I'd driven up its steep, narrow roads and encountered a magical sight—a family of moose crossing the street in front of me. As I sat there, watching, another car stopped on the opposite side, and there we sat, both of us at an impasse. The other driver cracked his window and stuck his cell phone out, snapping a few photos. He looked at me, and I looked at him, and we waited. A minute later, the moose trio crossed into a thicket of trees, and the wonderment was over.

Today the roads were clear and no moose were in sight.

I exited the off ramp and got into Nick's car.

"Took you long enough." He rested his hand on my shoulder. "How's the head?"

"No migraine today, so I guess I'm getting better."

He grinned, his dimples showing how pleased he was with his patient's progress.

"How did you manage to get an address for the boyfriend?" I asked.

"You're not the only person who knows how to *detect*. Did you have a good day?"

"Remember the girl I told you about, the one who ran out of Parker's Salt Lake home the other night?"

"The damsel in distress?"

I nodded. "I went to see her. I thought she needed to know the truth about Charlotte's death. Hopefully she'll steer clear of him."

"How'd that go?"

"I don't know," I said. "She wasn't much interested in talking and seemed a little nervous to see me. I just don't want anyone else to get hurt, not if I can prevent it."

"It wouldn't be your fault," he said. "There's only so much you can do."

"I'm obligated to these women. They need me, whether they know it or not, and I don't want to let any of them down."

"Do me a favor," he said.

"Yeah, what?"

"Catch your breath. I don't need you hyperventilating on me."

Until now, I hadn't noticed my breathing had changed. Hyperventilating wasn't something I did often, but occasionally, when my anxiety shot through the roof, I had to work to sustain it. I breathed in and out a few times until I felt a sense of calm.

Nick parked outside a dingy, rundown, three-level apartment complex. The dead grass along the front was covered in an abundance of cigarette butts. In its finest day the stucco exterior had probably been painted an attractive shade of white. Now it was a dingy gray color, with a surface that was crumbly, struggling to survive against the harsh elements of Park City's long winters.

We parked and exited the car.

"What are the odds he lives on the main level so I don't have to hike up these stairs?" I asked.

Nick laughed. "Slim to none."

We took the stairs to the third level, stopping in front of a door that had a brass plate on the outside, displaying the number three. The second number had fallen off leaving an outline of a nine in its place.

Nick knocked on the door.

A scruffy-looking kid cracked open the chained door and poked a bloodshot eyeball out. "Sup?"

"I'm looking for Bridget Peters," Nick said.

"What for?"

"We'd like to ask her a few questions. Can we come in?"

"You two cops or somethin'?"

Nick reached for his badge. I placed my hand on his arm. We exchanged glances, and he put his hand down.

"I'm friends with Audrey, Charlotte's sister," I said.

"Umm ... okay. Good for you."

"I wanted to see how Bridget is doing. I heard she took Charlotte's death pretty hard."

"Yeah, well, she's not here."

"When do you expect her?"

He shrugged.

"Mind if we ask you a few questions?" I asked.

"What for? Whatever you're after, it has nothin' to do with me, so you best be on your way."

Nick's jaw tightened the way it always did when he was irritated. He whipped out his badge and shoved it through the crack in the door. "Detective Calhoun. Open up."

"Aww shit, man, I got nothin' to say to you."

The door slammed. Nick pounded on it.

"I'm homicide, not vice," Nick said. "If I wanted to bust you for drugs, I would have done it already. You can open the door and let us in, or I can get vice out here to search your house. I suggest you open the door. *Now*."

The door remained closed.

"Please," I said. "It would be a shame if something bad happened to Bridget."

The door reopened.

"What are you talking about … something bad happening to her?" the guy asked.

"Let us in and I'll explain," I held out my hand. "I'm Sloane."

He glanced at my hand and laughed. "Whatever, lady."

"And you are?"

"Tommy."

Tommy's pupils were dilated.

We followed him into the living room. He bent over, picking up a plate of stale pizza off the floor. The band around his underwear reminded me of a Mark Wahlberg billboard from the early '90s. When Tommy stood back up, only part of his pants stood up with him. He grabbed both sides and yanked them higher. They slid back down again.

"I ain't got all day," he said. "You two gonna ask your questions or what?"

Nick took a notebook out of his pocket and flipped it open. "When was the last time you saw Bridget?"

"Yesterday."

"She didn't come home last night?"

"We don't live together," he said. "She's clean, and I'm ... well ... messy. It's better this way."

"We heard she was moving in with you."

He shook his head. "You heard wrong"

"Have you spoken to her since yesterday?" Nick asked.

"Naw, man. I've called her cell like a hundred times. I even left a message."

"And you weren't worried when you didn't hear back?"

"We got in a fight. I figured she needed to cool off."

"What caused the fight?"

He scratched the back of his head. "I mean it was stupid. She kept sayin' stuff like we needed to move someplace else—another town. Said she didn't want to be here no more. I was tryin' to reason with her, but it's hard to reason with your girl when she's flippin' out, right?"

"Why do you think she wants to move?"

"I don't know. She didn't say."

"And you didn't think to ask?"

"Look, man, when Bridget gets mad, I give her space so she can sort herself out. She always comes back."

What a winner the boyfriend had turned out to be. No wonder she'd left.

"What about her new job?" I asked. "I hear she went to work somewhere else."

"If she did, that's news to me."

"Yesterday, Bridget went to the real estate office. Any idea why?"

"She wanted to get her stuff. I drove her there. I waited in the car. When she came out, she was upset."

"Over what?"

Tommy shook his head. "You know, for a couple cops you two don't put much together, do you? Charlotte was Bridget's close friend, and now she's dead."

"So, Bridget was more than her assistant?"

"They met several years ago when Charlotte used to hook up with Bridget's older brother. They've been friends ever since."

Nick handed the notepad and pen to Tommy. "Write down Bridget's home address."

"I dunno if that's a good—"

"It isn't up for debate."

Tommy slumped back on the couch. "Fine, whatever."

He scribbled the address on the pad and handed it back to Nick. "Are we done here? I got things to do."

"Almost." I wrote my name and number on the notepad, tore it out, and handed it to Tommy. "If you hear from Bridget, will you let us know?"

He tossed the paper on the table without looking at it. "Yeah, maybe."

# CHAPTER 37

I tried calling Bridget, but there was no answer, just like the last time I'd called. The visit with Tommy had been bizarre, but we'd left with what we hoped was Bridget's address. It was something.

I typed the address he'd given me into the realtor database on my phone. "Now I know why I couldn't figure out where she lived before. She doesn't own the condo. Charles Peters does."

"The last name is the same," Nick said. "Charles could be her father."

"Let's stop by."

"And do what?"

"Take a look."

"I doubt you'll find her there. Seems like she's on the run."

I grinned. "Whether she's there or not, I'd still like to stop by."

He glanced at me and shook his head. "Oh, no you don't."

"Come on," I said. "I work for myself, so guess what? I don't need permission from you or the chief. If she's not there, what's the harm? Who's going to know if I let myself in for a few minutes and look around?"

He pointed a finger at himself.

I joined my wrists and held them out. "Why, Detective Calhoun, are you planning on arresting me?"

He wasn't amused.

I mapped her address and said, "Turn right up here."

"This isn't a good idea."

It wasn't a good idea. It was a great one. But I respected his desire to uphold the law and gave him an out. "You know what? Let's go home. I'll do this later."

"If you mean you'll go on your own the first chance you get, I don't think so. You check it out, and I'll keep watch. What's your plan for getting into her place, anyway?"

We made another turn, and the car came to a stop in front of a much nicer complex than the one we'd just come from.

I leaned over and kissed him on the cheek. "I'll find a way to get in. The less you know, the better."

There was only one person seated at the front desk when I entered, and his eyes were glued to an iPad sitting on his lap. He was around eighteen and had lustrous, long hair that belonged in a shampoo commercial. He closed his eyes, lifted his hands into the air, and whipped his head around, strumming to the beat of his air guitar. When the solo was over, he opened his eyes, gasping when he saw me.

"I wondered if you could do me a favor," I said. "I left my wallet inside my sister's place earlier today, and I seem to have lost the key card she gave me as well. It's been one of those days."

He removed his ear buds. "Who's your sister?"

"Bridget Peters," I said. "She's in unit 431."

"I'm not supposed to give another card out without her permission."

"You could call her," I said.

I gambled on the fact that if he did, she wouldn't answer.

He thought about it. "Yeah, I guess so."

He dialed the number and waited, and my gamble paid off.

"No answer?" I said. "She showed some houses today, and one of her listings was out of range. I have no idea when to expect her."

"Can't you wait until she gets home?"

"I'm headed out to dinner with some friends in a few minutes. And I—"

"You can't go without your wallet."

"Right," I said.

He hadn't been as easily persuaded as I'd hoped. I needed to change tactics. I leaned over the counter, looking at the device resting on his lap, and noticed he'd been watching a movie when I came in. It was paused. "What are you watching?"

"*Snatch*. Have you seen it?"

I nodded. "Such a good movie. I like the part where Brad Pitt is talking to the guy about dogs, and the guy can't understand what he's saying."

The kid laughed. "Pitt's the best part of the movie."

He set the iPad down, ran a plastic card through a machine, and handed it to me.

"Here," he said. "Go get your wallet."

I thanked him and walked to the elevator. My cell phone vibrated. It was Nick.

"How's it going in there?" he asked.

"Great, I'm in. Well, I'm almost in."

"Let me know if you need me."

"Ten four, over and out."

Bridget's place was downright pristine. There wasn't a speck of dust, dirt, or grime anywhere, and I was afraid to touch anything for fear I would ruin her perfectly sterile environment.

A bookcase in the living room contained a small DVD collection of black-and-whites, starring the late Marilyn Monroe. Propped up next to them was a photo of Marilyn from her early days when she'd still gone by the name Norma Jeane. She was sitting on an oversized green ball with a funny-looking starfish prop next to her, and her hair was a rusty shade of red and not the lustrous blonde she was known for later in life.

I continued down the hall and into the bathroom. The shower stall was dry. Bridget hadn't used it, not in the last several hours, at least. On the bedroom nightstand there was a photo of a girl I assumed was Bridget. She had straight, light-brown, shoulder-length hair and bright green eyes. Her arms were draped around Tommy's neck. The pair looked like the oddest couple, but she looked happy.

A duffle bag half full of clothes was on the bed. I riffled through it and found two pairs of jeans, a few shirts, socks, a pair of sneakers, and several pairs of panties. I unzipped the bag's side pockets and found travel-size shampoo and conditioner bottles, a bag of makeup, and a toothbrush and toothpaste.

Given the methodical order of Bridget's condo, leaving the bag there didn't seem to suit her personality. It was clear she'd intended on going somewhere. Questions flooded my mind. Why had she left the bag behind? What was her tie to the murder? Where was she now? And most importantly: why did it seem like she was on the run?

# CHAPTER 38

Maddie and I had just finished up with our jiu-jitsu class and changed back into our civilian clothes. Outside, snow flurried to the ground like soft, white feathers. We stopped next door for a hot beverage.

Maddie sipped her coffee and stared at the bandage on my head. "It's a good look. I like it."

"You can be honest," I said. "I know I'm a hot mess right now."

She laughed. "I don't know why, but I can't take my eyes off it. It's like passing a deer that's been hit on the road. You know you shouldn't look, but you do anyway."

"If you like this, you should have seen what I had to wear on my head the first day. It would have fascinated you for the rest of the month."

"How's your case going?" she asked.

"It's not."

"That good, huh?"

"I have learned one thing since I saw you last."

She leaned forward and lowered her voice. "Oh, yeah? What?"

"It's possible to move backward instead of forward on an investigation."

She sat back and frowned. "What if you don't solve it? Are you going to be okay with that?"

I glanced at her, sipped my tea, and said nothing.

"Oh, come on ... don't give me that face," she said.

"I have no idea what you're talking about."

"Sure you do. It's the same one you always give me when you don't like what I've said. I didn't suggest you give up. All I'm saying is, how long would you work a case you can't solve before you stop trying to solve it?"

Forever. It would become the thing that kept me up at night and ruined any chance of a decent night's sleep.

"I don't think of it in terms of giving up," I said.

"You allow cases like this to consume your life sometimes. You know that, right?"

"I just finished jiu-jitsu, and now I'm here with you having a drink. My cell phone isn't on me at the moment, and I haven't mentioned the case all day until now, until *you* brought it up."

She sighed and put her cup down. "All right. I'm just going to say it. You struggled today in class. You lacked focus. I know you, and I know what you're like when it comes to these jobs you take on. You'll push yourself until you're exhausted, and I don't want to see you go through the same thing you did when—"

She abruptly halted the conversation and pretended to stare out the window.

"Go ahead," I said. "Say it. You don't want to see me go through what I did when Gabrielle died."

"I'm sorry, I shouldn't have brought it up. It's not right. I'm sorry."

"No, it's okay. You, Nick, and everyone else all feel the same way. I get it."

"I understand how much you want to help this girl get to the truth about her sister. But she's not *your* sister, sweetie. She's not Gabrielle."

Maddie was right. Charlotte wasn't *my* sister. But she *was* someone else's, and that counted for something.

"Do you assume that's why I took the case?" I asked. "You think somehow if I can find Charlotte's killer, it's going to make up for what happened to Gabrielle? It won't. Nothing will."

"I didn't mean to upset you."

"I'm not. I ... can we talk about something else?"

She squeezed my shoulder. "I'm sorry. I mean it. Forget everything I just said. Okay? I'm shutting up now."

The snow flurries let up for a moment, and the sun beamed through the store window. I tipped my head toward the window and said, "That's my cue to head for the car."

Maddie finished her coffee, stuck a piece of gum in her mouth, and took her sunglasses out of her bag. "What's on the agenda for today? More pursuit of the bad guy?"

"Or bad girl."

"Bad girl ... I like it."

"I need to talk to Parker's other women. His so-called alibi flies in today, but there's someone else I need to meet with first."

We walked to the parking lot, but instead of heading to her car, Maddie went straight for mine.

"Forget where you parked?" I asked.

She pulled down her sunglasses, winked, and slid into the passenger seat. "I'm off work today, and I have nothing better to do. I'm coming with."

"Oh, you are, are you? I don't think so."

"Afraid I might badger your witness?" she asked.

"Or scare them."

"Into submission, maybe. And in that case, you need me. Oh, come on. You won't even know I'm here."

Bright-eyed, pigtailed Maddie dressed in a hot-pink tracksuit and furry white knee-boots wouldn't go unnoticed. In all the time

I'd known her, I couldn't recall a single occasion when she hadn't stood out. Ever.

"It's just that I'm better working alone," I said, "and I think it would be best if—"

"Come off it, Sloane. You're such a worrywart. Every good female hero who saves the day needs a sidekick, and I'm yours. Can you see it?"

"Can I see what?"

She brushed her hand through the air, painting an imaginary picture for me. "Two girls about town in their trusty 'Audimobile,' together on a mission to solve a heinous crime. It will be fun."

I tried to keep it together, but burst out laughing anyway. "Oh, all right. You can ride along today."

She fist-pumped the air.

"Promise to keep quiet and let me do the talking." I raised a finger. "I mean it, Maddie. Not a word."

# CHAPTER 39

The female Dynamic Duo, one dressed in a hot-pink tracksuit, and the other in faded jeans and a fitted sweater, rendezvoused at our first stop: Bridget's apartment.

I parked the car, opened the door, and looked at Maddie. "Stay here."

"I want to come, though," she said. "I'll behave."

"I just need to check and see if the girl who lives here has been home since last night. You can come with me at our next stop."

Maddie shot me a disapproving look and folded her arms, but she remained seated.

I crossed the courtyard and entered the building. A female was at the front desk this time. I smiled and held up my key card. She squinted, glaring at me like she wondered why she hadn't seen me before, but she said nothing as I passed.

I assumed Bridget wasn't at home but gave a courtesy knock just in case. When no one answered, I went in. Everything looked the same, all except for one thing: the duffle bag was gone. I had missed the chance to talk to her.

I walked back to the parking lot, disappointed. Before I reached the car, I spotted a green Honda parked at the far end of the lot. It was the same make and model Nick said Bridget drove when he'd checked with the DMV, and there was a person sitting in the driver's side. The car idled but didn't move. I walked over, taking my time. I didn't want to alarm her. When I got close enough to confirm it was the same girl I'd seen in the photo with Tommy, she put the car into gear, glanced behind her, and jerked the car backward. At twenty feet away, I wouldn't reach her before she sped out of the parking lot.

"Bridget Peters?" I yelled.

Her eyes widened.

"I'm a friend of Charlotte's," I said. "Can we talk? Please. I can help you."

Bridget's driver's-side window started to come down, but before I had the chance to say anything more a glimmer of pink sprinted past me. By the time the word *NO!* formed on my lips, Bridget had torn out of the parking lot like a bank robber making his getaway.

I glared at Maddie.

She shrugged and said, "Oops."

"*Oops*? You were supposed to stay in the car."

"I wanted to help. I'm sorry, I thought I could get to the car before she took off and—"

"And what?" I said. "She might have been the *one* person who could tell me what I need to know, and you've just scared her away."

We walked back to the car in silence. I started the car and pulled out of the parking lot. A few minutes went by in silence. I focused on the road, and Maddie focused on her lap.

Finally, she said, "I really was trying to help. You're right. I shouldn't have come."

And I needed to work harder on controlling my temper.

"Don't worry about it," I said. "I'm sorry I lost it on you. Something tells me Bridget's the key to all this, but she's afraid of everyone right now. I could see it in her face when I looked at her."

"Well, hopefully, this wasn't your only shot and you'll get another chance."

"I hope so," I said. "In the meantime, let's see what one of Parker's other women has to say."

# CHAPTER 40

It was midday when we pulled up in front of Zoey Kendrick's place. Her small, redbrick house looked old, really old, like it had been built in the late 1800s. Its miniscule size made it stand out amongst the newer grandiose houses on the street.

I pointed at the car parked in front of the house. "Looks like someone's home."

I got out of the car and glanced back at Maddie, who hadn't budged.

"The offer's still open for you to join me on this one," I said.

She tried and failed at hiding her excitement. "Really? Are you sure?"

I nodded.

She unbuckled her seatbelt. "I don't want to screw up anything else for you so I'm just going to keep my trap shut and let you do your thing."

We crossed the front yard and walked up to the door, and I tried to act like I didn't see the woman inside the house who had peeled back the corner of a crimson-red curtain so she could watch us approach the front porch. A few seconds later she disappeared, and the front door opened.

"Can I help you?" she asked.

"Are you Zoey Kendrick?" I said.

"Sounds like you two know who I am, but who are the two of you?"

"I'm Sloane, and this is Maddie," I said.

I handed her my card.

Zoey was dressed in a tank top and a pair of overalls, which were rolled up at the bottom. Her feet were bare except for a silver toe ring on the pinkie, and she had bits of what appeared to be dried orange paint on her face.

She glossed over the card I'd handed her with minimal interest and then handed it back to me. "Keep it. I don't need your services."

"Are you sure? You might."

She raised a brow. "What's that supposed to mean?"

"Can I ask you a few questions about Parker Stanton?"

"What about him?"

"A woman is dead, and I've been hired to find out what happened to her," I said.

She stood for a moment, trying to make a decision, and then pulled the door all the way open. "Come in, but I'm busy today. A few questions, that's it."

The inside of Zoey's house reminded me of a showroom. Modern art was represented on each one of the colorful walls. One painting had several pastel colors blended together in a swirled pattern. It hung on a red wall. Another painting was a series of vertical lines in neon colors. It hung on a blue wall. And the yellow wall in the dining room had a painting of a young girl scolding her cat.

"Wow, your house is amazing," I said. "It's so colorful."

She smiled. "Thank you."

I gestured to the painting with the swirl pattern. "Did you get this somewhere in town?"

She laughed and shook her head. "Come with me."

We followed her into a bedroom that doubled as an art studio. The floor was lined with canvas cloth and had splattered dried paint all over it. A table was set up in the middle of the room, with coffee cans filled with brushes resting on top.

"You painted all of these?" I asked. "Do you have a studio?"

"I'm not great at selling what I create." She grabbed a half-painted picture off of an easel—a mother looking at her newborn child. "My paintings are like children to me. I get attached to them most of the time. It's hard to give them up at any price."

"You do this for a living?" I asked.

"I live for a living. Art is one way I express that."

Maddie and I exchanged glances. Zoey's comment had been an unusual one. I wanted to dive in and pick her brain. The three of us walked back to the living room, and I sat next to Maddie on a vintage red sofa. Zoey sat across from us on an oversized, plush, purple shoe.

"All right," she said. "Let's get to your questions."

"I wanted to ask you about your relationship with Parker Stanton," I said.

"What about it?"

"Are you in one?"

She considered the question. "I suppose we are."

"How long have you been together?"

"The last few years, I guess."

Not days. Not months. *Years.*

"Did you know Parker was involved with Charlotte Halliwell at the same time he was in a relationship with you?" I asked.

"He told me they were engaged."

"You knew they were together?"

She nodded. "I did, and I encouraged it. She seemed good for him."

I was confused.

"It didn't bother you to be with a man who was also with someone else?"

"I've known Parker for years, long before he committed himself to Charlotte."

Zoey's candidness shocked me. It wasn't often I asked questions and received straight answers. I couldn't decide whether I found it refreshing or arrogant.

"Just to be clear, you knew about Charlotte, and you still continued to see him?"

She smiled. "That's right."

"Was your relationship with him an intimate one?"

"Is there any other kind?"

"If he married Charlotte, do you think he would have continued to see you?"

She grabbed a glass sitting on the table next to her, took a sip, and then reclined back in the chair. "Either of you care for some iced tea?"

Maddie shook her head. Zoey looked at Maddie and then at me.

"Does she ever talk?" she asked.

"Not if she can help it," I said. "She's mute."

"Is that supposed to be funny?"

"I don't know. Maybe. Can we get back to my question?"

She sighed. I was starting to lose her.

"Parker takes care of me. He pays for this house and gives me money for anything I need. We have an arrangement."

I imagined Parker thought he'd found the perfect woman in Zoey. No complaints, no restraints, no rules of any kind. All he had to do was peel back a stack of dollar bills, and he was free to wander in and out of her life as often as he liked.

"When you say *arrangement*, do you mean you don't mind that he sees other women because he pays your bills?" I asked.

"Yep. I get what I want, and he gets what he wants."

"Do you see other men too?" I said.

"Whether I do or don't, it has nothing to do with what happened to Charlotte, so why are you asking?"

"I'm curious. I'm not sure I've ever met anyone like you before."

She sat up. "Parker is my soul mate. It doesn't matter what I do or what he does. We're bound to each other. I get him. I understand him on a deeper level than any of the other women ever will. I'm sure he cared for Charlotte, but whether or not he loved her … I doubt it. She saw what she wanted in him. Maybe because he showed her what he wanted her to see, a side of himself, but not the whole person. With me, he had the freedom to strip everything away and be free."

"Charlotte wasn't the only woman he was seeing. There are others. Do you know about them too?"

She stared at me like I was the plainest, most vanilla cookie she'd ever met. "Doesn't it bother you that in today's society everyone follows a bunch of useless rules? One man and one woman. It's stuffy and restricted and so … blah. Why restrain yourself when you can live a life of complete openness with the freedom to do whatever pleases you?"

"What about physical abuse? Parker has been known to get rough with the other women. Does he hit you?"

She flinched. "When one person strikes another, you see it as a sign of abuse. I view it as an opportunity to let out pent-up frustration. It's a way to express oneself. When I throw paint against a blank canvas, I act out my emotions. It's how I create some of my most intimate art. I don't think of it in terms of abuse. I think of it more like—"

"Let me guess," I said. "It makes you free."

She nodded. "Exactly."

The conversation had taken a ludicrous turn. One look at Maddie, and I knew she was bursting to share some opinions of her own.

"Have you seen Parker since Charlotte died?" I asked.

I knew the answer to the question, but I asked anyway.

"We see each other whenever he has time. He comes and goes when he pleases."

"Has he spoken to you lately?"

"We talk all the time."

"About Charlotte's death, I mean."

"He's mentioned her. He's confused about why he's been implicated in her murder. I don't see what the police want with him, either. He's not guilty."

"What makes you so sure?" I asked.

"He's not capable of killing someone. Parker is an expressive person, but he would never end someone's life. And you ... you see a murdered woman, a victim, a killer who must be brought to justice in the name of the law. I see a woman set free from this life, given the power to roam the earth on her own terms. I hardly think you should waste your time feeling sorry for her. Wherever her spirit is, I'm sure she's happy."

Maddie grabbed my arm and squeezed.

"Thank you for your time," I said.

At the door, Zoey took my hands in hers and gazed into my eyes. "I see a lot of unrest in you. Go your way and embrace life. Don't live in the past. There's nothing for you there. It can't heal you. You must find peace within yourself and move forward."

"I ... uhh ... yeah ... okay," I said.

On the way to the car, Maddie slapped her thigh and burst out laughing. "First off, if this is what it's like being a private detective, I need to come with you more often. And second, why do I feel like I just returned from a seventies time warp?"

I shaped my fingers into a V, trying to keep a straight face as I said, "Peace and love, my sister."

# CHAPTER 41

I leaned back in my chair, kicking my bare feet onto the coffee table. Boo slept beside me. One of his eyes was open just a sliver. Every so often he'd grit his teeth and growl, and I wondered if he'd gotten any closer to catching the elusive kitty cat in dreamland.

I thought about Maddie's actions earlier that day. It was true what she'd said at the café. To some degree, Audrey's case had started to consume my thoughts. I didn't care. If I could catch her sister's killer, justice would be served, and the universe would align again. At least that's what I told myself, because then I wouldn't have to admit how much I needed the case to be solved in order to align things in my own world, righting the wrongs of past times where I had previously failed.

Nick walked into the room and said, "I just stopped by to see how everything was going before I head back to the station."

"You have to work tonight?"

He nodded. "The chief wants to brainstorm about what direction we should go in next."

"Sounds fun."

"I'd rather be here ... with you."

I wanted him here too, but I had a few plans of my own tonight.

"You and Madison stay out of trouble today?" Nick asked.

"I don't know where to begin."

He sat next to me. "You said something about that when you texted me earlier. How bad was it?"

"Probably not as bad as I made it out to be. When I texted you, we'd just left Bridget's place, and I was irritated. As the day went on, I realized it was nice to have Maddie there. She added an element of fun to the day. I'm sure I needed it."

"What happened at Zoey Kendrick's?"

"From the impression she gave me, Parker has an alternative lifestyle only she understands. She thinks they're 'soul mates.' And according to her, their relationship started years before he met Charlotte."

"If he was dating Zoey, why get involved with Charlotte?"

"So they could live as free spirits," I said, waving my hands back and forth in the air. "Peace and love and happiness, and everything's no big deal when you're high, right?"

Nick grabbed a wineglass off my nightstand and eyed me curiously. "How many of these have you had?"

"Just the one. I'm serious, Nick. Zoey knows about the other women, and it doesn't matter. Parker pays all of her expenses. She claims not to care about much of anything. It's like she could find out tomorrow that she was dying, and she'd throw a party to celebrate the life she was getting ready to have after this one."

"Did you talk to Zoey about Parker's abusive side?"

"She acted like she knows all about it. I got the impression she allows Parker to do whatever he wants to her. Parker presents himself as a different person to different people."

"Like a chameleon."

I nodded. "He does what suits him in the moment. With one woman, he's sweet and sincere and full of charm, and with another, he exercises complete control. Some come from money, some work for it, some hold a place in society, and others, like Zoey, scrape by on whatever they can get and aren't shy about asking for handouts. At least I have a good idea about how he keeps them invested now."

"How?"

"He starts the relationship out by playing the role of the perfect gentlemen until he gets to know the woman and what she's like."

"And then?"

"He mirrors them, altering himself accordingly so they feel comfortable. It works, for a while, until something sets him off and he fills with rage, and then the true Parker Stanton shows himself. By then, the women are whipped and so in love with him they stay until they break and can't take it anymore."

"Quite the theory."

"Here's another," I said. "Zoey's jealous of the other women. I don't care what she was trying to sell me. I could see it in her eyes. For all the 'free love' crap she claims to have, I believe jealousy is a side of herself she struggles with."

"Do you think Zoey could have killed Charlotte?"

"Maybe. Has anything new happened on your end?"

"Not really. Parker's alibi checks out. Kristin flew in this afternoon, and Parker brought her to the station himself so she could vouch for his whereabouts at the time of the murder."

"It doesn't mean he's not responsible. Parker has family money. Maybe she's lying for him or maybe he hired someone to do his dirty work so he didn't have to do it himself. I'm not about to give him a pass just because some woman says she's his alibi."

# CHAPTER 42

I sat across the street from Parker's house. Sooner or later, he'd emerge with his flavor of the weekend, and when he did, I hoped he'd take her to a nightclub or somewhere I could lure Kristin away for a few minutes and get some alone time with her, woman to woman.

I opened my glove box, fiddling around for a mint, and found a familiar piece of metal. I took it out, rubbing my finger across its cold, hard surface. Some people threw salt over their shoulders for luck, but not me. I carried my grandfather's old FBI badge. Looking at it now, it awakened memories of all the times he'd taught me to remember who I was and who I wanted to be. I wondered what he'd think of me now if he were still alive to see that I'd followed in his career footsteps, in a way. Would he have been proud? I wanted to think he would.

In my boredom, I tried calling Audrey. She didn't answer. Maybe it was for the best. I wasn't in a hurry to tell her Parker's alibi had checked out—and that I was no closer to finding out what happened to her sister than I had been a few days ago.

A car turned up the road, passed me, and then circled around. It crept along the other side of the street, turned off its headlights, and then parked a few houses away from Parker's. In the darkness, I couldn't see the driver, but I recognized the car. The man in black had returned for round two.

Parker's garage door opened, and his car reversed out of the driveway. I crouched down while he zoomed by, counting seven Mississippis before sitting back up again. Parker paused at the stop sign at the end of the street. I started my car, planning to follow him, but then my interest shifted to the man in black.

I put the car into gear and inched forward. The man in black did the same. With one hand on my gun and the other on the steering wheel, I crept beside him. His window came down, revealing a large, Frankenstein shape of a face that was rough and pocked. He had a three-inch scar on the side of his cheek. Whoever he was, it was clear he wasn't someone to be messed with.

"I don't know what you want with Parker, or why you're here, or why you left the note you did the other night," I said. "But I—"

I'd scarcely uttered the words before another car turned up the road, one I identified immediately.

The man in black looked at me and smiled.

"Who are you?" I said. "Tell me."

He winked, and without uttering a word, he stepped on the gas, taking off down the road.

The other car pulled up next to me, and I prepared for an even worse encounter than the one I'd just had.

"What in the hell are you doing here?" Coop said.

"Leaving," I said.

"I'm in charge of Parker's tail tonight. I don't need your help, and I don't need you sniffing around."

"Well, you're wasting your time. He's not here."

"I suppose you're going to tell me you know where he's gone."

"I might," I said. "But you don't need my help, remember?"

I put my window back up and breathed a sigh of relief. With

Parker long gone, the mystery man out of sight, and Coop hovering around, I called it a night. Kristin would be in town until the next day, giving me one last crack at talking to her.

I drove down the street and turned, and then my cell phone rang. I glanced at it to see who was calling, but the number was unknown. I pulled to the side of the road and answered it.

A desperate, quivering woman's voice said, "Stop following me!"

"I'm not sure what you mean," I said. "I'm not following anyone at present."

"Why can't you just leave me alone?"

"Who is this?" I said.

"Don't act like you don't know."

"I'd like to know who I'm speaking to, or this conversation is over."

"Then I have ... well ... nothing to say."

Unknown caller sniffled into the phone a few times, but remained on the line.

"Bridget," I said. "Is this you?"

There was no reply.

"If this is you," I said, "the only reason I stopped by your place is because I wanted to ask you a few questions. I'm not the police, and I'm not after you."

Another pause, and then she said, "If you're not following me, then who is?"

"I have no idea. Where are you? Do you need help?"

"I ... I don't know."

"Tell me where you are. Let me help you."

"I don't know you. Why should I tell you anything?"

"I'm sure Charlotte's death hasn't been easy on you. All I need is for you to help me catch her killer. If you're being followed, you need my help."

"I ... I don't know. I have to go."

"Wait, Bridget, please. Let's try this: I'll talk and you listen. You don't have to say a word if you don't want to, and you can hang up anytime. Deal?"

"I guess so."

"A couple of weeks ago, Charlotte's sister hired me to look into Charlotte's death. At first, it looked like an accident … until we discovered she was poisoned. I know you two were close. All I want to know is if you know why someone wanted her dead. I have my suspicions, but I haven't been able to prove them yet. Do you know anything that could help me?"

I let my words marinate for a moment and waited.

"You, umm, you said you have suspicions," she said. "Who do you suspect?"

*Try everyone from Parker Stanton to the evil troll lady in the dungeon of the real estate office.*

"Parker Stanton, but he has an alibi, and right now, the alibi checks out."

"Of course he does. He's Parker Stanton the third, real estate tycoon and multi-millionaire, blah, blah, blah. The boy who can pay his way out of anything."

"I take it you don't like him," I said.

"What's not to like? He's a rich, snobby brat who will stop at nothing to get what he wants. It's the Stanton way."

"The Stanton *way*?"

"He does whatever to whomever and doesn't care who he hurts in the process."

"Do you think he killed her?" I asked.

"Parker? No. He's just a grade-A sleaze ball."

Her response surprised me.

"How do you know it wasn't him?"

"Do I despise the guy? Yes. Is he a killer? I don't know. I don't see it."

I started to think she didn't know Parker as much as she thought she did. Then again, Vicki wasn't so sure he was to blame, either.

"Parker could have hired someone else to commit the murder," I said.

"I mean, maybe."

"Did he ever abuse Charlotte?"

"He was a little rough with her a few times."

"How do you know? Did Charlotte tell you?"

"She said a few things. Not much. I was the only one she confided in—about that, at least. She asked me not to say anything to anyone. The last time he hit her she had a few bruises. She threatened to break it off, and he never touched her again. But then she found out about his other women, and it didn't matter anymore. She was done with him."

"I know about the altercation between you and Parker at a real estate party a while back," I said. "Was it because you confronted him over the abuse?"

"I … it's complicated. I've already said too much."

The line went silent.

"Bridget, are you still there?" I asked.

I'd pushed too far.

She was gone.

# CHAPTER 43

"Why isn't anyone doing their job?" Audrey barked.

It was early, too early for anyone to be yelling in my ear.

"Calm down," I said. "We're doing everything we can."

I half-opened one eyelid and looked at the clock on my nightstand. It wasn't even six in the morning yet.

"At least I give a damn," she said. "I guess I'm the only one who does."

"Calm down, Audrey."

"Why should I? My sister is dead. No, let me rephrase that. My sister is dead because some scumbag murdered her, and said scumbag isn't locked up yet. I want to know why."

"The police brought Parker in for questioning," I said. "Without any solid proof, they can't hold him, at least not yet. He's still being looked at, and they're keeping an eye on him."

"What do you mean?"

"Trust me, Audrey. Okay? I'm sorry I don't have all the answers yet."

"It's been two weeks, and nothing has changed. Do you know how it feels to sit here and wait? Do you have any idea? He goes free while she rots in the ground. What kind of justice is that?"

I was tired and irritated. Her lack of patience and my lack of sleep didn't make for a winning combination.

"Two *weeks*. Not two months, not two years. It takes time. Think of it like trying to fit all of the pieces of a puzzle together. You get them all in place and find out one is still missing. One piece. Only one. And as soon as I find it, everything will fall into place."

"What about the cops? Do they share your sentiments?"

"I'd like to think so," I said. "Believe me, the more eyes we have on this the better. Give me some time to wake up, and I'll call you later. Sound good?"

I managed to find the button to end the call and rolled over to see a pair of eyes blinking at me.

"What's her deal?" Nick said. "Doesn't she know only an evil person wakes someone up this early on a Sunday?"

I pulled the covers over me and scooted next to him. "She hasn't got a patient bone in her body."

And with that, I fell back to sleep.

Morning came again a couple of hours later. I powered up my laptop, went to the Salt Lake International Airport website, and searched all flights with an arrival destination of New York City. I found three, the first departing in a few hours.

I grabbed a quick bite to eat with my two favorite boys and then headed to the airport. It had taken a good deal of finesse, but I'd managed to convince Nick a simple chat with Kristin required no accompaniment and that he needed to focus on his job, while I focused on mine.

The first flight came and went with no sign of Kristin or Parker. I took a gamble on the security gate she'd be at, hoping I'd chosen the one closest to the terminal for her flight. Thirty minutes later, it paid off. The two of them walked hand in hand toward the security gate. They hugged and kissed and hugged again before he walked away, pausing one last time to blow her a kiss.

What a charming little snake in the grass.

Kristin was a tiny woman, several inches shorter than I, and so petite she almost disappeared when she turned sideways. She had long, brown hair with blond highlights and big, blue eyes that reminded me of flying saucers. She didn't look like the others, but then, the others didn't look like the others, either. I imagined it was part of Parker's endgame—having one woman in every size, shape, and color. Buying ice cream must have been an impossible task. With so many options to choose from, how did he possibly ever limit it to just one?

Kristin looked like a woman ready to hit a day club in her bedazzled tank top, micro-miniskirt, and four-inch studded heels. She had a massive, fur coat draped over her arms, but given the rest of her wardrobe, it looked like it had been chosen more for its style than warmth.

I waited for her to take her place in line, fell in behind her, and tapped her on the shoulder.

"Are you Kristin Tanner?" I asked.

She spun around, glancing at my winter duds like she wasn't impressed. "Who wants to know?"

"My name is Sloane. Sloane—"

She aimed a finger at my face and shook her head. "Oh, no, no, no. I know who *you* are. Parker warned me about you. This is *not* happening."

"It *is* happening, though. I'm standing here, and you're standing here, and we're doing this whole conversation thing. Mmmkay?"

"What do you want?"

"I have a couple of questions. I promise you won't miss your flight."

She slung her carry-on bag over her shoulder, grabbed my arm, and jerked me out of the line. I shook her off, and we walked to an unoccupied corner of the room.

"I have nothing to say to you," she spat. "This is outrageous!"

"It's outrageous to ask you a few questions?"

"You followed me here. You're so … pathetic. You need to get a life, and stop meddling in ours."

"I needed to talk to you, and this seemed like the only way to do it."

"The only way *away* from Parker, you mean."

"If you say so," I said.

She placed a hand on her hip. "Well, you're wasting your time. Stay away from me, and leave Parker alone."

She spoke about him like she was his mother and I was the school bully who'd been slamming his face into his locker each day. *If only.*

"And if I don't stay away?" I said.

"Then if I were you, I'd watch your back. He's had enough of your shenanigans."

"I'll do whatever it takes to protect innocent women from a man like him."

"You're so stupid. You don't know anything. He's the best kind of man there is."

"Wow, he has *you* fooled."

It wasn't how I'd intended to conduct my question interview with her, but she seemed like the type of girl who required a steady amount of pressure to keep her engine going. One single, solitary slip-up was all I needed.

"I won't stand here another minute and listen to your outlandish lies," she said.

"You don't believe Parker cheats? Wake up and talk to any one of the hordes of other women he's seeing."

"Other women? How dare you accuse him of such a thing!"

She stood her ground, and I stood mine.

"I know you physically attacked him," she said. "You broke his fingers when you didn't get your way. You plan on breaking mine too?"

I hadn't, but slapping some sense into her sounded nice.

"I see he hasn't told you what actually happened between us the other day," I said. "I'm not shocked to hear he hasn't given you the whole story."

"You don't deny what you did?"

"It doesn't matter what I say now. Your mind's made up."

"He offered to help you with the investigation, even though he barely knew the poor woman who died, and what did he get in return? Harassed and physically assaulted. You should be ashamed of yourself."

"And you shouldn't be so naïve," I said.

"What's that supposed to mean?"

"The woman you say he *barely* knew? She was his fiancée. They had been in a relationship for two years."

Kristin shook her head. "You're so full of it."

I reached into my coat pocket, pulling out the photo of Parker and Charlotte that I'd lifted from Charlotte's house. I tried handing it to Kristin, but she jerked back in horror like I was handing her a knife dripping in blood.

"There are other women too," I said. "At least two besides Charlotte."

She fought herself not to look at the photo so I held it even closer. She glanced at it for a second and then looked away. When she turned toward me again, her eyes were blurred with tears.

"You're a liar," she said. "So they were in a photo together. Big deal. They were just good friends."

"You don't believe that though, do you? Not deep down. Somehow you know what I'm saying is true, and if you don't know, you at least suspect it is. My clients pay me to uncover the truth, and that's what I'm doing. You need to stay away from him."

"Because if I don't he'll, what? Kill me like he allegedly killed her? Get real."

"Maybe he won't kill you," I said. "But at some point he'll hit you, if he hasn't already. That's how it all starts. Was he even with you the day Charlotte died or are you lying to protect him?"

Her eyes bored into mine, and I imagined she was ramping up for her next sassy comeback. Instead, she pivoted on her studded heel, making a beeline for the security gate.

"I hope you enjoyed your time with Parker," she said. "You won't get any more of it."

"Why? Is he going somewhere?"

Kristin showed her boarding pass to the security person and glanced back at me before passing through the gate to the other side. "You're the private investigator. You figure it out."

# CHAPTER 44

I ran a few errands in town and then took Boo for a walk along the Rail Trail. He scampered down the path, sniffing old friends along the way and making some new ones. We passed a much larger, mangy-looking, black dog that resisted a bond of any kind. Boo got close enough to invade the black dog's personal space, and the dog sounded the alarm. Boo, oblivious to his actual height or lack thereof, steadied his approach, much to the chagrin of the dog and its owner, who shook her head at me like I was an unfit parent. Boo didn't seem to care, and neither did I. He wagged his tail and did a few spins for his newfound friend, and we continued on our way.

Forty-five minutes later, I was feeling refreshed and bold, and I decided it was time to speak to Parker again in person. I arrived at his house and stepped out of the car to the sound of something rustling in the hedges in Parker's front yard. I crouched beside my car and waited. The sound came again, except this time it was followed by movement. I pulled my gun from its holster and switched on my flashlight, aiming the beam in the direction of the sound I'd heard. When I opened my mouth to verbalize a warning, a large mass of fur leapt over the hedge, skipped across the street, and faded into the night.

After the deer encounter, I took a moment to catch my breath and then crossed the street to find Parker's front door open, just wide enough for a person to stick their hand through. I called his name into the darkness, but the only response I received was a reverberation of my own voice. I aimed my flashlight toward the windows of the garage and glanced inside. His car was there, so where was he?

I entered the house and walked into the living room, tripping over a pair of men's shoes that had been left out on the floor. Once I stabilized myself, I moved farther down the hall until I reached the master bedroom. A large mass of something was lying on the floor. The flashlight revealed it was nothing more than the duvet from Parker's unmade bed.

"Parker? Are you here?" I said. "It's Sloane. Your front door was open, so I came in. We need to talk."

I walked to the opposite end of the house, entering a room that looked like his office. The desk was barren with the exception of a few folders and a single piece of folded paper, which was sitting in the middle of it. I picked the paper up and unfolded it. Scrawled in pen were two words: *forgive me.*

Forgive me?

What had he done now?

The paper slipped through my fingers, falling to the floor. I bent down to retrieve it and slipped on a wet, sticky substance. I pushed my hands in front of me, trying to break my fall, and my hand swept across something hard as I hit the floor. The hard object slid to the side, making a sharp noise that sounded like the blade of a knife cutting across cement. I pulled myself to my knees and bent down to investigate, placing my hand on the armrest of the chair for balance, but the leather on the chair didn't feel like leather at all. It felt like flesh. Cold, clammy, wet, human flesh.

I jerked my hand back and flashed the light toward the chair.

There sat Parker, his body slumped over to one side. I turned around, aiming the beam from the flashlight on what I'd felt on the floor. A gun. I reached out, feeling Parker's neck for a pulse. There wasn't one. I reached inside my pocket, grabbed my phone, and pressed number one on my speed dial.

"Nick," I said in a whisper. "I'm at Parker Stanton's house. I think he's dead."

# CHAPTER 45

"What were you doing in his house?" Nick asked.

I shook my head and stared at the floor.

"When the chief gets here, he'll want answers," he said. "If you talk to me, maybe I can talk to him, and you won't have to deal with it. Well, you won't have to deal with it yet, anyway."

I nodded. It was all I could do at the moment, and even that seemed like too much. My body felt like someone had taken a stick and smacked my funny bone over and over again. But there was no humor in being the one to find Parker's dead body.

"Sloane, listen to me," Nick said. "Look at me."

I hesitated.

"Would you look at me please?" he asked.

I removed my hands from around my knees and sat up. Nick had a bewildered look on his face like he couldn't decide whether to scold me or comfort me.

"You're shaking," he said. "It's going to be okay. *You're* going to be okay."

"I think I'm in shock."

"That's natural."

I wiped my eyes. "I shouldn't have come here. I can't believe he's dead, Nick."

"Do you know how it happened?"

"I found him on the chair. I don't know how he got there, only that it had to be in the past few hours because he was at the airport before that. There was a paper on the desk with a couple words on it, and a gun on the floor, and he had no pulse."

I looked down at the dried red smudge marks on my shoes and wanted to vomit.

"I want to talk to you about this," he said, "but the other guys from the police station are on their way, and I don't want anyone to see you like this."

"Too late." Coop glanced at me. "I see you've already messed up my crime scene."

"Go easy on her, Coop," Nick said. "She's been through hell tonight."

"She's the one who decided to enter the house without permission. You want to tell me what went on here?"

"Don't say a word," Nick said.

Coop glared at Nick and then shifted his focus back on me. "The way I see it, you and Mr. Stanton fought, he went for his gun, and you shot him. Am I right? He was a twerp. Can't say I blame you."

"Enough," Nick said. "You know that's not what happened."

"Son, I'm not talking to you."

Nick's ears turned bright red. "I'm not your son, and we both know she's under no obligation to say anything to you."

Coop and his flared nostrils made a move for Nick, and they squared off. "Now you listen here—"

I jumped off the floor, wedging myself between them.

"Enough!" I said. "I'll talk, but only to the chief."

# CHAPTER 46

"Sloane and I will speak alone in my office, Calhoun," the chief said. "You wait outside."

Nick acknowledged him with a nod and left the room.

The chief shut the door and then his blinds before walking around to his side of the desk. He didn't sit down. He just stood there for a minute, pulling at his moustache.

I rested my hands on my lap, staring down at one of my fingernails. It was broken, but I would have preferred to stare at it all night than make eye contact with the chief.

"All right, Sloane, out with it," he said. "Let's hear what you have to say."

"Is this my official statement?"

"Someone else can do that later. Right now, all I want to know is what happened from start to finish. Think you can manage it?"

I nodded and started by filling him in on my meeting with Kristin at the airport. I told him about the comment she'd made at the end, the one that had caused me to go to his house—her words suggesting he was planning to skip town.

"But Kristin didn't actually *say* he intended to leave?" he said. "Right?"

I shook my head. "It was the way she said it, like she wanted me to know he was getting ready to take off and we'd lose him."

"All right, what happened next?"

"I went to Parker's house and—"

"Stop right there," he said. "I asked you to keep your distance. Does anything I say matter to you?"

"At the time, it seemed like a good idea."

"You broke into the guy's house," he said. "I could hold you for that."

"You won't."

He gripped the sides of his desk like he wanted to snap it in half. "A few nights in a cell might do you some good. Maybe you'd listen to me for a change."

I had crossed a line, and he wanted me to know it.

"I thought you had a tail on him," I said, "but no one was around when I got there. I looked. Where were they?"

He mulled it over for a moment, knowing it was a fair point.

"Don't change the subject," he said.

"At least I'm trying to catch Charlotte's killer."

He shook his head. "You think that's what you're doing, eh?"

"I don't have the energy to go back and forth with you," I said. "Not today."

He stood, folding his arms in front of him. "Continue on with what happened next."

"When I got to Parker's house the lights were off, but his front door was cracked open. It just seemed weird. His car was in the garage, and the lights were—"

"Skip to the part where you went in."

"I thought if I could find something, anything, to prove Parker's involvement in Charlotte's murder, you could arrest him."

"You're so foolish sometimes, kiddo," he said. "No matter, I suppose. What's done is done. You went into his house and found him dead. Then what?"

"I called Nick."

"And that's it?"

"Almost. I did find a note on his desk, which you already know about."

"Yeah. Wonder what his *forgive me* crap is about."

He looked toward the ceiling, muttering the words over and over a few times, thinking.

"The note is referring to one of two things," I said. "Either he was confessing to killing Charlotte, which I'd like to believe, or he was confessing to something he'd done to someone else, to another woman, perhaps."

"You say it like you don't believe the former is true. Isn't this what you wanted, to catch him and prove he killed her?"

"It's just that I never thought Parker of all people would off himself," I said. "It doesn't make sense."

"In what way?" he asked.

"Parker slept with a lot of women. On the outside, he was selfish and full of himself and proud. On the inside, he was an insecure coward who got his kicks by controlling those around him. You and I both know a gunshot to the head doesn't fit the profile—not for him."

"What would you suggest happened? You're obviously thinking something."

"Let's say Parker really did want to die for what he'd done. Why not take a bunch of pills and take the easy way out?"

"You ever consider you might be overthinking it a bit?" he said.

I shrugged. "It wouldn't be the first time."

He sat down at the desk and sighed. "The gun was convenient and easy. I hear what you're saying. We'll see what forensics has to say."

# CHAPTER 47

Three days had passed since Parker's death, and I'd spent the majority of it at home. I wanted to avoid any run-ins with Coop, who felt I had tainted *his* investigation. I received no thank-you for discovering the body, no words of appreciation, nothing for my efforts. It seemed everyone had accepted it was all over. Parker killed Charlotte and then killed himself. Or so it seemed.

My cell phone rang. It was Audrey.

"I got your message," she said. "I can't believe it's all over."

"That's the general consensus."

"Parker did himself and everyone else a huge favor. He got what he deserved."

I didn't see any point in debating with her at the moment, so I didn't.

"What's next for you?" I asked. "Any big plans?"

"I'm out of here."

"For how long?"

"Maybe for good. It's time to move on with my life. This town reminds me too much of Charlotte. It's hard to drive around and still see a few real estate signs with her beaming face on the front and keep telling myself she's really gone. They'll all come down eventually, but I feel like I can't move on unless I leave."

I'd felt the same way about my sister's death a few years earlier, except Audrey was leaving for the same reason I'd decided to stay.

"Will you ever come back again?" I asked.

"I don't think so."

"Any idea where you'll go?"

"Do you want to know something interesting? A couple of days ago, I was looking through Charlotte's mail, and I came across a letter from a woman in Haiti. She said she was looking forward to Charlotte and her sister arriving next month to assist with the reconstruction project they'd started there. I mean, I didn't even know about it, but what a great opportunity, right? I want to go, to honor her, and create a memory we aren't able to have together."

"When will you go?"

"You might think I sound crazy, but I'm leaving today."

"Wow," I said. "I think that's great."

"Imagine my surprise when I realized Charlotte never planned to transfer to another real estate agency. She wanted to leave this place, and she was going to try to talk me into going with her."

"I'm sorry I never got the chance to meet your sister," I said. "Sounds like she was an amazing person. If there is anything you need—"

"There is one thing you could do for me."

"Name it."

"I put Charlotte's home on the market. I've sent some movers over to pack it up for me. In the meantime, I've listed it with Vicki. I'm on my way to the airport, and I don't really have time to drop the key off. Since I gave you a copy, I hoped you could stop in and give her yours?"

I ended the call feeling excited for her and the journey she was about to embark on. The news of Parker's death had given her peace of mind again. I could hear it in her voice. Why didn't I feel the same way?

Boo's ears perked up as Nick walked in with dog treats in one hand and daisies in the other. He opened the bag and placed a treat on Boo's nose.

"For the lord," he said.

Boo wiggled his nose, snatched it up, and looked at Nick for a second. Much to his dismay, Nick turned toward me and extended the flowers.

"For the lady," he said.

"What's the occasion?"

"Do I need one?" he said.

"I guess not."

He wrapped his arms around me. "We've dropped the case. The medical examiner's report came back, and it's conclusive. Parker committed suicide. The latent prints we lifted from the gun matched Parker's, and no other prints were found on the weapon."

"Sounds too good to be true."

"There is one caveat, though."

"What is it?"

"Before the ballistics report came back, I ran the serial number on the gun. It's not registered, and Parker's father said his son didn't own a gun. If that's true, where'd he get it?"

"He was a resourceful guy. I see your point, though. What about the note he left behind? Did you confirm he wrote it?"

"We compared the suicide note to some handwritten papers found inside his desk. They matched."

I put the daisies in a vase, walked over to the couch, and sat down. "I can't believe it. I guess it's really over."

"At least now you can put it behind you and move on."

I shrugged. "I guess so."

I wanted to feel a sense of relief, but something bothered me. I thought about the man in black and couldn't shake the feeling there was something we didn't know.

# CHAPTER 48

An hour later, I sat on a black velvet sofa shaped like a peanut and tried to forget it was a mere nineteen degrees outside as I scooped a spoonful of chocolate gelato into my mouth.

Maddie took a bite of wildberry and pointed her plastic spoon at me. "You're so quiet today. What's your deal?"

"I'm fine."

"No, you're not. Don't make me pry it out of you. You know I will."

"I planned on spending today without thinking about Charlotte or Parker or the case, but the harder I try *not* to think about it, the more I do."

"Why think about Parker at all? The douchebag extraordinaire is dead, and aside from his father, and a woman or five, I don't see too many other people around who are unhappy about his demise."

Maddie finished the last bite of her gelato and set her bowl on the table, not seeming to care about the remnants of melted gelato dripping from her container onto the table. She didn't notice, and since it was her bowl, I tried to ignore it. I lasted a whole five seconds before snatching a napkin from the dispenser and wiping it up.

"I remember something," I said.

Maddie sat straight up in her chair. "Is it salacious? Do tell."

"Parker was left-handed."

Her eyes widened. "Fascinating. What's the exciting part?"

"That's it."

"That's a few spoonfuls shy of a juicy scoop. What made you think of it?"

"The first time we met in the lobby of his place downtown, he handed me a flower with his left hand. And then later in his apartment, he held a glass in his left hand. When he pinned me up against the wall—"

"I get it, left hand."

"I broke the fingers on his left hand," I said.

"Help me understand where you're going here."

"The report said Parker shot himself with his right hand."

She bent her head to the side. "Who knows, maybe he's ambidextrous."

"And maybe I'm the new Princess of Wales," I said.

"What did the coroner's report say?"

"Nick said the results were conclusive: Parker shot himself. They found no other prints on the gun, and there's no way I can get access to the report. The chief has me on some type of time-out while Parker's dad is in town, investigating what happened to his son. I mean, I get it—the chief's just doing what he needs to do. Besides, I don't know what made him madder—me breaking into Parker's house or the fact I discovered Parker's body before they did."

Maddie walked over to the water dispenser, filled two cups, and then returned to the table. "*You* can't gain access to the report. Maybe I can. Who's the coroner?"

"I'm not sure about the first name. The last name is Whitley."

"Stan Whitley?"

"I think so. Do you know him?"

She grinned. "Do I ever."

"Now it's your turn to spill."

"He has a bit of a crush on me."

I shot her a wink. "Doesn't everyone?"

"Oh, give me a break," she said. "You can have any guy you want."

"The having isn't the problem, though, is it? It's the holding. It makes me feel ... I don't know ... trapped, I guess."

"I think you're scared."

"And you aren't when it comes to commitment?"

She laughed. "That word isn't part of my vocabulary. I'm not the marrying kind. I have no interest in a long-term relationship."

She didn't now, but there was a time when she'd considered it with a man named Ben, whose fondest wish had been for the two of them to wed. Maddie had almost agreed until he revealed his plan for what she'd be doing *after* the wedding—staying home to make a tribe of little Bens. He thought somewhere in the four-to-six range seemed good. Maddie wanted a career, which for Ben, was a deal breaker.

"You thought about getting married once," I said.

"I ran into Ben a few months ago. Did I tell you?"

"You didn't."

"He was with his pregnant wife and their three bundles of joy. The bundles were running amuck like a bunch of crazy kids in *Children of the Corn*."

She'd always had a bit of a dramatic flare, but the visual imagery made me laugh.

"How long has he been married?" I asked.

"About five years now, I guess."

"Nick wants to move forward. He wants to make it official. He wants us to move in together."

"You can't blame him for asking, sweetie."

"Right now, our life together is simple and uncomplicated. I have my space, and he has his. It's perfect the way it is."

"For you. Not for him. What are you on, your second year together?"

I nodded. "We just hit the two-year mark."

"No wonder he wants to settle. If you two were both in your twenties, it would be different. You're almost double that, so …"

"I thought you of all people would understand," I said.

"Just because I don't plan to walk down the aisle doesn't mean you shouldn't. My motto in life is that you only get one. Don't waste it."

"You think I should go for it?"

"No, I'm not saying that. If your gut is telling you to hold off, you should listen. I like Nick. He's a great guy. I'm just not sure he's the right guy for you."

"You've never told me that before."

She smiled. "You never asked."

I still hadn't, even though I appreciated the honesty.

The door to the ice cream parlor swung open, and a group of teenagers strolled in, speaking at such a high decibel I was sure I'd rupture an eardrum if we stayed. Maddie glanced back at them, rolled her eyes, and we both reached for our coats.

"We were never like that, were we?" I said.

"Sadly, I think we were. We were probably even worse. Well, I know I was."

"Hard to believe."

We walked outside.

"Headed back to your office?" I asked.

She shook her head and smiled. "Not yet. I believe I'll stop in and catch up with my old friend Whitley."

# CHAPTER 49

When I was a young girl, not even a teenager yet, I had a master plan, a vision board locked away in a safe place inside my head, and whenever I took out my key and visited, I'd add a bit more to my life plan. Grow up, get married, and raise kids—four of them to be exact. Two boys, two girls. I'd even named the children: Piper, Kelly, Rhys, and Trevor. Problem was no one ever told me what to do when my master plan failed, and I was too headstrong to believe it could be anything less than what I imagined. I would have a perfect husband, raise four perfect children, and live a perfect life.

But then I grew up, like we all did. Marriage came, followed by divorce, and the dream of four kids? It never happened. Plan A didn't work out, and I never thought I'd need a Plan B.

Maybe Charlotte felt the same way. On her vision board, she'd aspired to greatness. She was a professional skier and then a successful real estate agent. She met and fell in love with a man who she thought she could trust, and at some point along the way, she became cognizant enough to realize he didn't have her best interests at heart. I wondered if she had been in a good place in her life when she died. She'd paid the ultimate price and was taken much sooner than she should have been. It didn't seem fair.

By the time I reached the real estate office, the *Closed* sign dangled from the front door. No key for Vicki tonight. I looked up her number and gave her a call to see what time she'd be in the following day, and she asked if I could bring the key to her house. She had a client anxious to see the place and wanted to do a walkthrough beforehand to see what needed to be done before she allowed any prospective buyers inside.

So much had changed in so little time. One day Charlotte was alive, and the next, the condo was about to be sold to the highest bidder.

I arrived at Vicki's house around dinnertime. She stood at her front door with a wineglass in one hand and a remote control in the other.

"This is a nice house," I said. "Are you married?"

"I was. My husband and I divorced a couple of years ago. He lives in Florida now on his yacht with a woman half his age."

"Sorry to hear it," I said.

She shrugged. "Don't be. I got the house, and he got the tramp."

"Oh, I see."

She took a sip of wine. "Sorry. That was a bit crass. It's just … when he cheated on me, it came out of nowhere. I was blindsided. It was humiliating. And though it was a while ago, I guess I still harbor unresolved feelings. It makes me feel better to get a snide comment in here and there, but I know it doesn't make it right."

"I don't mind. How's life at the office these days?"

"Almost back to normal, if you can call it that. Jack is back to his old self again, pushing us to get those numbers up … sell, sell, sell."

The brisk winter air swept across my face, and I shivered. "I'll be right back. I need to grab my coat in the car."

"I'm sorry. How rude of me. I'm standing here in the doorway talking to you, not realizing you're freezing. Come on in for a minute."

"Thanks for the offer, but I can't stay."

I reached for the key in my purse and handed it to her.

"I heard what happened to Parker on the news," she said. "Sounds like you closed your case."

"Audrey is satisfied, and everyone wants to move on with their lives."

"And you?"

"I don't know, and I'm not sure it matters anymore. It's convenient for everyone to assume Parker killed Charlotte and then himself when he couldn't live with the guilt of her murder. I'm just not convinced it's as perfect as it appears to be. Who knows? Maybe I'm overthinking it."

I ran my hands up and down my arms.

"You sure you don't want to come in?" she asked. "A glass of wine will warm you right up, and I'd love the company. Gets a bit too quiet in this house sometimes."

"I have plans tonight. Thanks again, though."

"All right, then … if you're sure." She flipped the key over and over in her hand. "It was good to see you again, Sloane. Thanks for this."

# CHAPTER 50

Maddie called the next morning.
"How's Whitley?" I asked.
"Much improved," she said. "It was a long night, for both of us."
"Did you get anything out of him?"
"Really, Sloane, what do *you* think?"
"Should I ask what you had to do to get it?"
"Probably best if you didn't."
Something crunched in the background.
"Care to know what's in my hot little hand right at this moment?" she asked.
"Not Whitley, I hope."
She laughed. "And people don't think you're funny."
I had my moments.
"We need to talk," she said. "Can we meet at your office?"
"Sure. Thirty minutes?"
"Yep. See you then."
When I pulled into the parking lot, Maddie was already waiting, which surprised me since she wasn't the most punctual of people. We walked inside, and she handed me a file.

"Merry Christmas," she said.

I smiled. "And a Happy New Year to Whitley."

"Oh, no you don't. Don't look at me like I've just done the walk of shame. I know all about what you've had to do for information."

I ignored the statement and sat down. "Did Whitley *give you* this file or did you pinch it?"

She smiled. "You know something? Home-office copy machines are so much better these days, so much quieter than they used to be."

"Well, I appreciate your efforts, criminal or otherwise. Thank you."

She glanced around. "You got any drinks around this place?"

"There's a bottle of pinot in the cupboard, if that's what you're after. It is a bit early for wine, though."

She gave me a disapproving look, walked to the cabinet, and poked her head in. "What a mother lode! You think you have enough tea in here, because I'm sure there's a village in some third-world country that could survive at least a month on all this stuff."

"Not funny," I said.

She raised her hands like she'd just surrendered. "I got it. I got it. Don't mess with a woman and her tea."

I walked over and nudged her out of the way. "Here, let me look."

She stepped aside.

I pushed the tea to the side and pulled out a bottle from the back. "Baileys?"

She nodded. "Excellent."

I poured her a glass. We returned to the desk, and I set the file down and opened it.

"Have you looked this over yet?" I asked.

"Yep."

"And?" I asked.

She leaned in like she was about to share the combination to a secret government locker.

"I think you were onto something, yesterday," she whispered.

"Look through this. Tell me what you see."

I opened the file. "What I see will be different than what you see, though."

"Even so, I'd like to know your take."

I sighed and went through the papers she'd copied, line by line. "Based on the report, he committed suicide just like everyone thinks he did."

"Right, but it doesn't add up."

"What doesn't?"

"Any of it."

"I see," I said. "And why are we whispering?"

Maddie glanced at me like she hadn't realized her voice was lowered and then she reclined back in the chair. "Good point. Here's the thing. On paper, the report holds up to snuff for anyone who looks it over and doesn't know any better. I get why none of it sounded an alarm at the police station. The way it reads, Parker shot himself, end of story."

"You just said it didn't add up. What are you seeing that's different?"

"Oh, don't get me wrong. The report is conclusive. He killed himself." She stabbed a finger onto the report. "If you read this, you'll be convinced Parker shot himself. Because that's what *they* want you to believe."

"You've lost me," I said. "Who's *they*?"

"I don't know. I can't say for sure. That's what *you* need to figure out."

I hoped at some point she started making some sense ... or any sense at all.

"I'm confused," I said.

She leaned in again, and we were back to whispering. "It's okay. I have a theory. I don't think Parker killed himself, but I believe someone wants *you* and everyone else to think he did. It took a few glasses of brandy last night, but I got Whitley to talk, at least enough to get one thing out of him. And Sloane, it's good. It's really good."

"Maddie, I get you're revving up for a big reveal, but out with it already."

She crossed her arms and grinned. "It seems our esteemed Whitley is on somebody's payroll."

# CHAPTER 51

It turned out Whitley had spilled a lot more than a few splashes of brandy on the rug. He told Maddie that Parker hadn't killed himself, and that it had been set up to look that way. Maddie, in her one-night-only starring role as Whitley's desirable temptress had done her best to talk him into giving her a name. It was to no avail.

What if Parker hadn't killed Charlotte and hadn't killed himself? It would have been easy to assume the same killer had killed them both, but it wasn't logical. Aside from the fact both murders looked like they'd been staged, the crimes were committed in very different ways. It didn't make sense that a killer would poison his first victim and shoot the other.

In the short time I'd known Parker, I'd come to understand how someone like him could have potential enemies: a jealous girlfriend, someone outraged enough at Charlotte's death to seek revenge, or maybe an old flame from the past.

And then there was the mysterious man in black. Who was he, really?

I turned onto the freeway headed toward home and checked my rearview mirror. For the last four miles, I had been followed. At first, I chalked it up to coincidence, but the longer I drove, the more I didn't think so. And given the pathetic job the person behind me was doing of hiding, I was certain I was dealing with an amateur.

I still had seven miles to go before I reached my exit. I stepped on the gas and moved into the left lane, passing a few cars in the process. When I reached the exit ramp, I checked my mirrors. The car wasn't there.

Seconds later, the same car I had seen before barreled off the ramp toward the stop sign. At the rate it was going, I thought it would miss the stop sign altogether, but at some point the driver realized the road came to an end and slammed on the brakes. The car lurched back, expelling gray fumes into the air before coming to a complete stop. I kept one hand on the steering wheel and felt around for my cell phone with the other. I picked it up and held it to my ear, but it didn't make a sound. I looked down, realizing my charger wasn't plugged in all the way.

My phone was dead.

Instead of continuing to my house, I decided a public place was the best option. I headed toward the gas station. The car followed. I pulled into a stall. The other car parked a few stalls away, and the driver's-side door opened. I tucked my gun beneath my jacket, opened the door, and slid out, crouching down beside the car so I could see my stalker approach. Five feet away, then four feet, then three, and then I saw the silhouette of a woman with her hands stuffed inside her coat pockets.

"That's far enough," I said.

She stopped. "Miss Monroe?"

The voice sounded familiar. "I know you've been following me. Show yourself."

"It's me."

"Stop with the games," I said. "Who's *me*?"

"It's Bridget. Please, I need to talk to you."

I stood up but kept to the side of my car. I had to be sure it was her. "Let me see your hands."

"My … hands? Okay."

She removed her hands from her jacket pocket, palms up.

"Why the hell are you following me?" I asked.

"I'm sorry, I'm so sorry. I didn't mean to freak you out. I called you, but it kept going to voicemail. I left you a ton of messages, and then I saw your car back there and recognized it from the other day. I tried to get your attention, but you didn't see me, so I figured I would follow you. Not the best plan, I know."

"You still haven't told me why you've decided to talk to me now," I said.

"I didn't know who else to call or what I should do."

"About what?"

"I went to my place this morning to get a few more of my things."

"Where have you been staying?"

"At a hotel in Heber."

Heber was about a thirty-minute drive from Park City.

"Why are you staying in a hotel?" I asked.

"I'll tell you. But first, when I stopped at my condo, some of my personal items were broken, and my files were scattered all over the floor. I took one look at the place, and I took off."

"Was anything missing?"

"I … I'm not sure. I didn't stay long enough to find out."

I walked toward her. Her eyes were bloodshot. I put my hand on her arm and she leapt backward.

"I'm sorry. I've been so jumpy today." She looked at her hands. "I can't stop shaking."

"It's all right. I know where we can go."

She nodded.

"And Bridget," I said, "I think it's time for you to tell me the truth."

## CHAPTER 52

Boo took one look at Bridget and barked, letting her know she was an unwelcome stranger in his domain.

"Forgive him," I said. "We don't get many visitors. He's only like this at home. At the office, anyone can walk through the door and it doesn't bother him."

Bridget approached Boo, stretching out her hand. He inched forward, giving her a closer inspection by sniffing her hand, and then he growled and backed up again.

"Oh, Boo, stop it," Nick said, entering the room.

Bridget flinched. "I ... umm ... I thought you said you lived alone."

"I do. But I take in the occasional riff-raff from time to time."

Bridget wasn't pleased.

Nick held out his hand. "I'm Nick, and you are?"

She looked at his hand with reluctance. "Bridget."

Nick glanced in my direction, trying to conceal the shocked look on his face. I stared back at him but said nothing. And I didn't need to. For all the trouble I had with verbal communication, one nonverbal look told him everything he needed to know.

"If you two would excuse me, I think I'll give you some girl time," Nick said.

"Don't leave because of me," Bridget said.

"Actually, I have a plane to catch." He thumbed in my direction. "I just stopped by the say goodbye to this one."

"When does your plane leave?" I asked.

"Two hours. Walk me out?"

I looked at Bridget. "Help yourself to anything you'd like in the kitchen, and I'll be right back."

We walked outside. Once we were out of earshot, he said, "How did she end up here?"

"Long story. I'll tell you all about it later."

"I have a few minutes. Give me the highlights."

I did.

"Why would she come to you instead of filing a report with the police?" he asked.

"I don't know all the details yet. All I can tell you is she's afraid of whoever is after her, and she decided to come to me."

He rested his hands on my shoulders. "The murder investigation is over, Sloane."

"What about the information Maddie found?"

"All Maddie has is the word of a guy who got drunk and blurted out a bunch of random comments. It doesn't change what's in the report, and it doesn't make it fact. Even the copies she gave you don't prove anything. He probably made it all up so he'd seem a lot more interesting."

It was the one part of our relationship that always brought me to a standstill. Nick's overprotective nature always favored my safety over me putting myself in danger of any kind. I didn't blame him, but sometimes it came with the job.

"I don't know, Nick. I don't think so. Someone trashed Bridget's place."

"Whatever is going on with this girl, it doesn't change anything.

She has a drug addict for a boyfriend. Maybe he messed up her place looking for cash. Let the cops deal with it."

He kissed me goodbye and walked away. He was taking a quick trip to Arizona to help a college buddy shop for the perfect ring for his soon-to-be fiancée, but it was still long enough for Nick to return with a little wedding fever of his own.

When I reentered the house, Bridget had made amends with Boo, who was resting peacefully beside her on the couch. I joined them.

"Look," I said, "I need to know what's going on."

She stared at Boo and remained silent.

"You want to know something?" I said. "I don't believe Parker killed Charlotte. And you want to know something else? I don't think my case is over yet. I don't care how many people were fooled by what appeared to happen at Parker's house. And whether you choose to help me or not, I *will* discover the truth."

I gave her some time to think it over.

"I don't believe Parker killed Charlotte, either," she said.

"Do you know who did?"

She shook her head.

"Then why couldn't Parker have done it?" I asked.

"Because she told me."

"Who told you? Charlotte?"

"She told me, and now she's dead."

"Bridget, what did Charlotte tell you?"

She rubbed her hands up and down her jeans.

"You're safe here," I said. "You can talk to me."

Tears pooled in her eyes. "Don't you see? Charlotte found out, and someone killed her. They killed her! And now they will come after me."

"Why will someone come after you?"

She bolted off the sofa. "This was a mistake, I can't stay here. I should go."

I raced after her, catching her at the door. "I want to help you. Will you at least give me a chance?"

"And when you do, someone will come after you too."

"You came to me for a reason. Don't give up on me now."

She stood at the door with her hand wrapped around the knob, ready to exit. I backed off, giving her the space I knew she needed. Some time passed, and then she calmed down enough to release the door and return to the sofa.

"How about you ask me some questions, and I'll try to answer them?" she said.

"All right. Let's talk about the night at the office party when you and Parker got into an argument."

"It's not what you think."

"What happened, then?"

"I wasn't arguing with him over Charlotte. Parker hit on me."

"Like, he asked you out?" I asked.

"Worse. He sent a disgusting photo of himself to my phone, and when I didn't respond to it, he approached me and asked me to come back to his place after the party was over. He said he sent the photo so I could see what he was going to *give me* later."

The thought of it turned my stomach.

"How awful," I said.

"Do you want to know the worst part? He was at the party with Charlotte, and he actually thought I would consider his proposition and not say a word to her about it."

"What did you tell him?"

"I slapped him across the face, and I left."

"Did you tell Charlotte?"

She nodded.

"Then what happened?" I asked.

"Charlotte didn't say a word to him at first. She hired a friend of hers to follow him and see what else he'd been up to that she didn't know about."

"When you went back to the office the other day, why were you so upset when you left?" I asked.

"It was just being there. A couple months ago, Charlotte got a wild hair, and she asked me to organize all of her files in the office by creating a spreadsheet to keep track of all their sales."

"Charlotte's and Vicki's?"

She nodded. "I created a template, and we started going back through all the transactions for the past year. I logged several of them, and it was going fine, until Charlotte came across a few files that had some problems."

"How so?" I said.

"I'm not sure. She just said she needed to check on some things and that she was going to talk to our broker to see what was going on. She asked me to save what we had already done, and then she took a few of the folders with her and told me to file the rest."

"And she gave you no indication about the problem she'd found?"

She shook her head. "The night before Charlotte died, she called me. She'd decided to leave Park City. She felt her life was going in another direction. It was the happiest she'd sounded in months. Before we got off the phone, Charlotte said there were two things she had to do before she left: talk to her sister and meet with the real estate board."

"I'm guessing she didn't go into details about either one?" I asked.

"She didn't. She just said she didn't want to involve me any more than necessary. But she did make an unusual request."

"What did she ask?"

"She wanted me to stay away from the office until I heard from her."

I thought about the files I'd found at Charlotte's house on the night of my attack. They hadn't seemed important at the time. If only I'd known they were.

"It's too bad I can't get my hands on the copies of those files," I said.

Bridget hesitated a moment and then reached into her pocket and pulled out a key ring. Two keys dangled from it. "Actually, you can."

# CHAPTER 53

I followed Bridget to Tommy's apartment. He wasn't home. She left her car along with a note saying she was all right and would return later. Then she got in the car with me.

We parked across the street from the real estate office and headed over.

"My key should still work," Bridget said.

"What do you mean, *should*?" I asked.

"Every time an agent or an assistant quits or goes to work for a competitor, they change the locks. It's been so crazy since Charlotte died, I'm hoping they haven't done it yet."

"You could have mentioned this before."

She shrugged. "We still would have driven over here to find out."

She inserted her key into the front door and turned it to the right. It clicked.

"We're in," she said.

The television was playing the same looped video montage. The light from the screen offered just enough of a glow for us to reach the stairs before I had to click my flashlight on.

We walked to the filing office, which required a different key to open it.

"Uh oh," she said. "We have a problem. This key isn't working. Now what?"

"Let me take a look," I said.

I wasn't shocked the woman with the troll-doll obsession had changed locks after I came sniffing around, but it was a cheap, standard doorknob, and jimmying it open wasn't much of a challenge. One twist from a standard paperclip and we were in.

"*Voila*," I said.

"Not bad. I'm impressed."

I handed her the flashlight. "Your turn."

Bridget located the files and handed them off to me. We headed back up the stairs, coming to an abrupt stop when we heard what sounded like a car parking in front of the building. The front door to the office opened, and someone walked in.

I turned to Bridget, whose jaw had dropped open like she was prepared to scream. I placed a finger to my lips, motioned for her to ease back down the stairs, and clicked the flashlight off.

Upstairs, a male voice said, "I know these people personally. They lost everything when their business went under last year. One more month on the market without a good offer, and they'll accept anything thrown their way. I'm sure I can convince them to do a short sale."

"It's Jack," Bridget whispered.

"Sounds like he's on the phone."

"What are we going to do? He can't find us here."

"All we can do is keep quiet for now and wait it out."

Jack continued talking. "Sure, sure. I understand. Let me just grab the file, and I'll tell you what your counter offer should be."

The basement light flickered a few times and then came on. We slid behind the door at the bottom of the stairs, but it wasn't big enough to conceal us both.

Jack stopped on one of the stairs and said, "Oh, wait a minute.

You know what? I just remembered something. I was looking at that file yesterday. I believe it's still in my office. Let me find it, and I'll call you back."

He walked back upstairs and turned the basement light off, and we relaxed in the darkness.

"What if he comes down here again?" Bridget said. "What if he sees us? What are we going to do? We need to get out of here."

I gripped her arm. "Keep it together. It's going to be fine."

She flinched like she was preparing to make a move, and I applied more pressure.

"Ouch, that hurts," she said.

"I'm sorry, but I need you to stay put. If you don't, there's a good chance you'll get caught."

A few minutes went by before we heard Jack's voice again.

"I think somewhere in the ballpark of eight and a half is a fair offer," he said. "I'll write everything up and get it over to you tomorrow. All right then, Talk to you later. Buh-bye."

The office door opened and closed, and for the next several minutes, we remained still, giving him ample time to get in his car and drive away before we walked to the main level and peeked out the window.

"Good," I said. "Looks like he's gone. It's late, and I could use another pair of eyes on these reports. I'm not exactly sure what to look for. Why don't you stay at my place tonight?"

"I don't know. Tommy must be worried. I've never been gone this long without calling. I was just trying not to involve him before I figured out what I should do."

"Why didn't you go to the police?" I asked.

"And say what? I didn't have any proof of anything."

"Still, when you learned Charlotte's death wasn't an accident, you could have at least told them your suspicions."

"I just wanted to get out of here. I probably sound like a jerk, like I didn't care about Charlotte enough to tell anyone what I knew."

"You were scared," I said. "People aren't rational when they're consumed by fear. Can I ask you a personal question?"

"Sure, I guess."

"What attracted you to Tommy? You two seem so different from each other."

"I get that question a lot," she said. "I've known him since we were kids. His life hasn't been the easiest, and he's still trying to figure himself out, but he knows me better than anyone."

"Then you should call him and let him know where you are. Stay the night at my house, and tomorrow I'll drive you home."

# CHAPTER 54

I got Bridget squared away in my guest room and then settled into my own bed and opened the files. From the size of the stack I had to sort through, I could tell the past year had been a fruitful one for both Charlotte and Vicki. I considered waiting to look at them until morning when Bridget could help me, but I was wide awake, and I knew I wouldn't get any sleep knowing the files were sitting on my nightstand.

Step one in my sorting process was to separate the transactions according to agent. I arranged them into three piles that consisted of Charlotte's deals, Vicki's deals, and the deals they shared together. In the past year, Charlotte had closed forty-six transactions. No wonder the other agencies had fought over her. Of those, five were shared with Vicki. Vicki herself had a modest year, with twenty-four transactions. I looked over Charlotte's files, but nothing stood out to me that was unusual. The same could be said for the shared deals she worked on with Vicki.

I laid both sets of files next to me, leaned back, and rested my head on the back of my headboard. The moon shone through my window, and I imagined it must have been past midnight by now. I closed my eyes and thought about how nice it would be to drift off to sleep, but I still had one more pile of files to sift through, and I wasn't a quitter.

I wrapped a robe around me and went to the kitchen, surprised to find Bridget sitting on a barstool, staring into the bottom of a cup of coffee.

"Can't sleep?" I said.

She nodded.

"Coffee will only make it worse," I said. "I'm making some tea to help me wind down. Want some?"

She shook her head. "Nah, I'm fine. I don't feel like sleeping, anyway."

"Me neither. I took a look at some of the files."

"Find anything?"

"Nothing out of the ordinary so far."

I poured some water into the kettle and set it on a burner on the stove.

"Why don't you just nuke it?" she said.

"I don't mind taking the time to heat it up."

We sat in silence until the kettle hummed. It was a well-worn kettle, one I'd used so much there were dime-sized wear marks on every side, and the spout put up a good fight every time I flipped the handle to pour the water out, just like it was doing now.

Bridget stared at me in disbelief. "Man, using a kettle seems like a lot of work."

"I thought so too when I first used it," I said, "but it was a gift from my sister."

"I've got a couple of sisters myself so I know how it is. I bet she checks to see if you still use it when she comes over here."

"Actually, she passed away," I said.

"Oh, I'm sorry. Were you two close?"

"We were," I said. "She was my only sibling."

"Did she get sick or something?"

I shook my head. "I don't talk about my sister very often."

"It's that painful?"

I cupped my hands around the mug. "It is. She was murdered."

The cup Bridget had been drinking from slipped through her fingers, shattering along the tile floor. She jumped off the stool, knelt down, and began picking up the pieces.

"I'm so sorry," she said. "I've broken your mug. Tell me where you got it, and I will get another one for you."

I scanned the floor, walked to the other side of the room, and grabbed the broom.

"No need to be sorry," I said. "I sprung the comment about my sister on you, and I shouldn't have. Sometimes I don't know the best way to talk about things, and I end up blurting things out, which usually proves to be the worst thing I can do."

"You're just being nice. It was my fault. I kept going on and on, asking questions about her, and now look at what's happened."

I scooped the broken pieces into the dustpan and dumped them into the trash.

"Your sister probably gave the mug to you too, and now I've gone and broken it," she said.

"I picked it up at the outlet shops for a buck. It's no big deal."

I hadn't, of course, but she'd suffered enough guilt for one night.

I grabbed Vicki's files from my room and returned to the kitchen.

"Since neither of us wants to sleep," I said, "what do you say we take a look at this last set of files? I could use your help."

She nodded.

I divvied them out, and we went to work. Seven transactions later, I noticed a pattern. "Is it common practice for your clients to use the same appraiser for every deal?"

"It depends. If a specific appraiser isn't requested, there's a list of people we recommend. Why?"

"So far, every one of these properties used Walker Appraisal, LLC."

"That's Travis Walker. Vicki uses him a lot."

"What about Charlotte?" I said. "Did she go through him too?"

"Maybe once or twice in the past year, I think."

I found seven more deals with Travis Walker listed as the appraiser. I wasn't sure what to make of it, but fourteen sales with the same appraiser in a town with dozens of appraisers to choose from attracted my attention. I handed them to Bridget to look through.

Fifty-five minutes and one more cup of coffee later, she closed the last of the files and turned toward me. "Do you have a computer?"

I retrieved my laptop from my room, and she typed in the address for the real estate listing service.

"What are you doing?" I asked.

"I'm trying to log on using Charlotte's username and password. Hopefully, it will work."

She pulled up the home page.

"What are we looking for?" I asked.

"I can't say for sure, but Vicki's listings were remodels, and I want to take a look at the history of each property to see what I can find."

Bridget clicked through a few of them, and then her eyes lit up.

"There! Right there," she said.

"What have you found?"

"I had a hunch the properties had all been flipped recently, and I think I'm right." She turned the computer screen toward me. "Look at this. All three of these listings were bank-foreclosed homes, and all of them sold to the same client before they went back up on the market a few months later. I bet if we look at the rest, they'll all be the same too."

"Flipping homes is legal though."

"Most of the time. Not always. It depends." She pulled one of the files out, opened it, and handed it to me. "It doesn't make total sense to me yet, but something seems off."

"Like what?"

She pointed to the picture in the file. "A few days before Charlotte died, she was talking to Vicki about this listing and said it needed to be fixed or made right or something. Vicki agreed. Charlotte wasn't mad or anything, so I just assumed a simple mistake had been made. Now, I'm not so sure."

Over the next hour, we pored over the files Travis Walker was involved with. It turned out they were all bank-foreclosed homes or short sales, which the purchaser bought cheap, made some minor changes, relisted, and sold through Vicki.

Bridget yawned.

"Let's both turn in for what's left of the night," I said. "We can pick this back up again in the morning, and I'll see what I can find out."

She nodded, slid off the stool, and walked down the hallway, stopping before she entered the bedroom. She turned and looked at me. "Hey, Sloane?"

"Yeah?"

"Would it be okay if I asked you one more question?"

I recognized the inquisitive look on her face. It was the same one I'd seen countless times before when I talked to people about Gabrielle.

"The answer is no," I said. "The police didn't ever catch my sister's killer."

## CHAPTER 55

Tommy was seated outside on a plastic chair when I dropped Bridget at his complex. As soon as he saw her sitting in my passenger seat, he smashed the joint he was holding into the snow and walked over. She got out, and they embraced.

"I missed you, baby," he said.

"I'm sorry," Bridget said. "I should have told you everything from the start."

He brushed a tear from her cheek. "You're here now. Nothing else matters."

She glanced in my direction. "Let me know what you find out today, okay?"

"Will do. Stay here with Tommy and keep yourself safe until you hear from me."

She nodded and headed toward the stairs.

Tommy leaned into the car and smiled, and for the first time, I saw a softer, gentler side of him. "Thanks for bringing her back to me, lady. We cool?"

"We cool," I said. "Take good care of her."

He fisted his hand and held it out in front of me. It took a few moments for me to realize what he was doing, and then I remembered seeing other teens doing the same thing. I made a fist, and we bumped. It was a simple gesture, but for a moment, it made me feel young again.

I backed out of the parking lot, took out my cell phone, and dialed. A chipper, young female voice on the other end of the line said, "Ellis and Marshall Real Estate. Can I help you?"

"I'd like to speak with Vicki Novak, please," I said.

"She's not in the office at the moment."

"When do you expect her?"

"I'm not sure. Can I take a message?"

I declined, ended the call, and turned the car around, deciding on a new course of action.

# CHAPTER 56

I entered the office of Walker Appraisal right before noon. A girl, maybe mid-teens, was sitting behind the desk, eating a plate full of mini donuts. Her cell phone was glued to her hand, and she didn't look up when I came in. I walked to the counter, hovering over her just enough to disrupt her from the text she was sending.

She looked at me, annoyed, and said, "Can I help you?"

"I have an appointment with Travis Walker," I said.

"He's not back yet." She used her cell phone to direct me toward a row of chairs against the wall. "You can sit there and wait for him.

I sat. She swiveled her seat around so her back was facing me and then went back to texting again.

So much for hospitality.

Ten minutes later there was still no sign of Mr. Walker.

"Excuse me," I said. "Do you have any idea where he is at the moment?"

She looked back at me and shook her head.

"Can you find out?" I asked.

She grunted, tossed her cell phone to the side, picked up the office phone, and placed a call. Several seconds later, she hung up.

"He didn't answer," she said. "I don't know what to tell ya."

It was easy to see why Charlotte rarely used his services.

Now that the girl's cell phone was out of her hands, I decided to take advantage of the situation.

"Have you worked here long?" I asked.

She rested her elbows on the table and stared at me. "Off and on. I'm just helping out with the phones, I guess."

"Vicki Novak referred him to me. Do you know her?"

Her eyes widened. I'd piqued her interest. Good.

"Is she a friend of yours?" she asked.

"Not really. She's just someone I know. Why?"

"Vicki Novak's a home-wrecking B word. I hate her."

It wasn't where I'd thought the conversation would go, but I wanted to keep her talking, so I brought the conversation down to her level and climbed aboard the "B" train.

"Vicki and I were supposed to do a couple of real estate deals together," I said. "Then I found out she talked to my clients behind my back, and now they're listing with her. I haven't spoken to her since. How do *you* know her?"

It wasn't the most elaborate lie I'd ever told, but it seemed good enough.

"I don't know her. Not really. My dad does."

"Who's your dad?"

She pointed to the sign on the door, displaying the name of the business. Travis Walker was her dad.

It made perfect sense now.

"I take it your dad and Vicki were involved?" I said.

She nodded. "Yep. My parents never had any problems until Vicki came in here one day asking him to do some appraisals for her, and then she started calling him all the time. One night, he didn't even come home, and when I got up the next morning, my mom said he'd already left for work, but I'm not stupid. I knew he was with *her*."

If the kid was right, and Vicki had destroyed the marriage, it made Vicki no better than the cheating ex-husband she'd complained to me about.

The cell phone on the desk vibrated. The kid reached over, typed a message, and then tossed the phone back down again.

"Does your dad still see Vicki?" I asked.

She shook her head.

"What about your mom?" I asked. "Are your parents back together now?"

"My dad moved out, and my mom filed for divorce last week."

"I'm sorry," I said.

"The only reason I'm here is because my mom is trying to force me to spend time with him, but he's always taking off. And when he is here, he acts weird around me because he knows I know what he's been doing."

The office door opened and in walked a tall man around my age who looked like he fasted more than he ate. He also struck me as the kind of guy telemarketers considered gullible prey.

His eyes darted from his daughter at the desk to me.

"Are you my twelve o'clock appointment?" he asked.

I nodded.

He shifted the notebook he was carrying from one hand to the other and stuck his hand out to me. "Good. I hope you haven't been here long."

"Twenty-five minutes or so. Are you in the habit of making your clients wait?"

He stared at me, taken aback by my frankness, and I just smiled. I was only at a level one. I hadn't even turned on the heat yet.

"I'm sorry," he said. "I hope I haven't messed up your day."

I stood there, staring at him. There was nothing like a few moments of awkward silence to get things moving in a different direction.

He pointed down the hall. "Why don't we step into my office?"

I nodded.

If his office offered any indication about his own personal style, he was in dire need of one. Everything was brown, from the walls to the worn, outdated carpeting.

"What can I do for you?" he asked.

I got straight to the point.

"You can tell me how you came to work for Vicki Novak," I said.

"I'm sorry? I don't understand. I thought you came in on behalf of a client who needs some appraisal work done."

"We have a mutual client in common. Charlotte Halliwell. Do you know her?"

His face soured. "I didn't work with her much. It was unfortunate, what happened to her."

Unfortunate? I could have thought of a thousand more descriptive words.

"And Vicki Novak?" I said. "How often do you work with her?"

He broke eye contact and shifted positions in his seat. His discomfort was telling. I reached into my bag, pulled out the files, and dropped them onto his desk. They made a slapping sound.

"What can you tell me about your dealings on these listings?"

He glanced at the files, staring at them like they were a disease he needed to get away from, and then he leaned back in his chair and crossed his arms. "You think if you chuck a few files on my desk I'll tell you privileged client information?"

"Who have you been falsifying information for—Vicki Novak, or her broker, Jack Montgomery?"

"You're out of line."

"Am I, though? I spent most of the night poring over these files. I'm tired, and you're busted, Mr. Walker. You may as well come clean."

He threw his hands up. "I think you have me confused with someone else. You should go."

"Right," I said. "I'm the one who's confused. And I suppose you were never romantically involved with Vicki, either."

"Of course not!"

"Funny, your daughter seems to think so, and apparently, so does your wife."

"My daughter doesn't know what ... my personal life is ... it's none of your business."

I grabbed the files off his desk and stood. "I'll save myself from any further denials on your part and take these to the real estate board. I'm sure they'd be thrilled to help me sort everything out. Nice meeting you, Mr. Walker."

I turned for the door, and he stood and said, "Wait."

## CHAPTER 57

Travis picked up the phone and pressed a button. "Courtney? Why don't you go on home for the day, honey? I'm going to be longer than I thought. I'll take you to a movie tomorrow. I promise."

He hung up the phone and buried his hands in his face.

"Let's start over, shall we?" I said. "I'll go first."

I tucked the files back into my bag and sat down. "I am a private investigator, and I was hired to look into the murder of Charlotte Halliwell."

He sighed. "Figures."

"Now you go," I said.

"Straight to prison."

"Prison?"

"You're here, which means you know already."

I didn't, but I was glad he thought I did.

"Why don't you indulge me for a moment and talk about it?" I said.

"You women never let up. What do you want to know about first—business or personal?"

"I'll take business for a thousand," I said.

"Fine. About six months ago, Vicki contacted me. She'd heard good things about the work I'd done in the past, and she wanted me to do a couple of appraisals for her. If she was satisfied with my work, she promised to start using me on a regular basis. I helped her with a few deals, and everything went well."

"And then what happened?"

"She asked me on a date. She didn't know I had a wife, and when I told her, it didn't seem to make a difference."

"So you went out with her?" I asked.

"Not at first. I said no the first few times. She just kept asking. She wouldn't take no for an answer. Being with her was the worst mistake of my life. I've lost everything that ever mattered to me over it."

I nodded, because he had.

He cleared his throat. "I need … just a second."

He stood up and walked out of the room, and for a moment, I wondered if he was going to take off on me. A minute later, he returned holding a bottle of water. He twisted the cap off and downed the entire thing. He tossed it into the wastebasket and leaned against the wall. He looked rough, and it was about to get rougher.

"If Vicki coerced you into doing something, and you're innocent in some way, maybe I can help," I said.

"No one can help me now. It's too late. I've lost my wife, my daughter, and my business. You don't understand. I wanted to get out. I told her I wouldn't do it anymore."

I still wasn't clear on what he'd done. I pressed for more information.

"When you denied her anymore help, what did she say?" I asked.

"She told me I needed to keep my mouth shut if I didn't want to be taken down with her. She threatened to tell my wife everything, which worked at first, until I realized my wife already knew."

"Why didn't you come clean then?"

"Vicki is crazy, and I don't mean a little crazy. I mean a lot. A couple of weeks ago, she tried to run me off the road. I confronted her about it, and she said it would be tragic if my daughter was driving and something awful happened to her. I shouldn't have allowed her threats to silence me, but I did."

"Do you know who murdered Charlotte, Mr. Walker?"

Beads of sweat formed along his brow. "I don't know. I mean I have my suspicions. I can tell you I didn't have anything to do with it, though. I swear."

On the corner of the desk was a photo in a frame. I presumed it was his family. I picked it up and looked at it for a moment. They all looked so happy, like most people did when they posed for a family portrait. *Smile for the camera, and we'll all pretend not to show any of our cracks.* I wondered about his life before Vicki had entered the picture and destroyed it. I tried not to care. I knew whatever he'd done, he'd brought it on himself. Still, I felt compassion, not so much for him, but for his wife and daughter.

"You have a lovely family. It's a shame this has happened." I placed the picture frame in front of him. "Don't you owe it to them to come clean?"

He stared at the photo for some time and said, "I shouldn't have allowed it to go this far. I thought if I kept my mouth shut, it would all resolve itself. I could have my life back, the life I had before Vicki destroyed it. She played me, used me like some worthless piece of garbage, and all for what—a few bucks? It makes me sick."

"Tell me what she did, and I'll make sure she doesn't get away with it," I said.

"What can you possibly do for me now? It's too late."

"I can connect you with the right people. Help me, and I'll promise you two things. I'll make sure Vicki goes to prison for a long time, and I'll speak in court on your behalf. You may not be innocent, but it seems like you're not as guilty as she is. Do we have an agreement?"

"I guess." He clenched his hands together and stared down at them. "One night, Vicki told me she had a great business proposition for me. She said if I wanted in, there would be decent money in it for me. She had an investor who would buy any home she offered him. All we needed to do was flip it and make a profit. I wrote the appraisals, and she took care of the rest."

"Sounds legitimate," I said. "I don't see the problem."

"The appraisals were fraudulent."

"In what way?"

"Vicki would find an investment property, usually a short sale or a foreclosed home."

"Or someone desperate enough to sell," I added.

He nodded. "Vicki's investor fronted the money, and then once she closed the deal, we waited about four months, and she relisted it."

"Let me guess," I said. "You relisted it for a significantly higher amount."

"We hired someone to come in and clean, maybe slap on some paint and make a few changes, but in the listing, we fudged the truth."

"How so?"

"Vicki had a way to make a hundred dollars of work look like several thousand."

"Are you saying most of the changes and upgrades she said she'd done never took place?"

"It depended on what shape the house was in. She would hire guys on the cheap to make a few fixes to certain items that were easily noticed, and then she would lie about other items that weren't visible in a walkthrough. I chose comparable houses in the area that were higher-end so Vicki could market the listing at an inflated price, making the purchaser think they were getting a much better deal than they actually were. And because I signed off, there was never any question about the validity."

"And the money?" I said. "Where did it go, in her pocket?"

"Vicki gave me a small cut and kept the rest for herself."

"Was the investor in on the scam?"

"That's the most interesting part of all of this. A couple of months ago, she admitted there was no investor. The money came from a trust fund she'd received after her parents died. She'd blown through most of it, and this scheme of hers was a way for her to maintain the lifestyle she'd grown accustomed to when she was married."

"How did she manage to pull the deal off without anyone there to sign?" I asked.

"Most homes in Park City sell to people who live out of the area, so she forged the signatures, and at closing, she produced a document granting her attorney-in-fact privileges on behalf of the investor."

"Wouldn't the title company realize she used the same method at every closing?"

"Vicki used a different company every time, and if they ever needed to call and speak to the investor, when they dialed the number Vicki gave them, it rang through to me."

"What was Charlotte's role in all of this?"

"She didn't have one. Charlotte and Vicki had their own listings and only worked as a team on listings that were priced over the million-dollar mark. Vicki made sure the homes she purchased were less, so it never raised any suspicions."

"But Charlotte found out, didn't she?" I said.

He nodded.

For the first time since taking Audrey's case, my thought process was clear. The phone call Audrey had received from her sister saying she needed to talk to her about something most likely had nothing to do with Parker and everything to do with Vicki. From what I had learned about Charlotte, she would have never stood by while fraud was being committed, whether she was friends with her partner or not.

"I appreciate your honesty," I said.

"There is one more thing I need to get off my chest before you go. Charlotte came to see me. She knew what we'd been doing, and she said it needed to stop. She told me she had always thought I was a good guy, and she wanted to give me the opportunity to do the right thing and turn myself in before she did."

"I'm guessing you told Vicki. Right?"

He lowered his head, providing me with the answer.

"You have to believe me. I didn't know anything would happen to Charlotte at the time or I never would have said a word."

"When did you tell Vicki?"

He paused a moment and then said, "Two days before Charlotte died."

# CHAPTER 58

I left Travis's office and called Nick. It went to voicemail, and I suspected he was on his return flight home. I sent him a text and then got into the car and made another call.

The call was answered, "Park City Police Department, Rose speaking."

"I need to speak with Chief Sheppard," I said.

"He's in a meeting right now," she said. "Shall I tell him to call you when it's over?"

"Rose, this is Sloane. Do you know when he'll be free? It's urgent."

"They've been at it for at least an hour already, so I bet they'll wrap it up soon. Can someone else help you?"

For a split second, it crossed my mind to talk with Coop. Then the second passed.

"Please tell him to call me the second you see him," I said.

"Sloane, you're not in any kind of trouble, are you?"

My phone beeped. "I have another call coming in, and I need to take it. Please have the chief call me right away. Okay?"

I clicked over to the other line, and Tommy yelled, "She's gone!"

"Calm down, and tell me what happened."

"I just got out of the shower, and Bridget isn't here."

So much for my advice and her staying put.

"Did anything happen between you two?"

"Nothin' much. We were ... uhh ... spending some alone time in the bedroom and stuff and then Bridget said she was hungry. She said she was gonna grab her bag out of the car, change clothes, and make us lunch while I showered."

"Is her car still there?"

"Hang on, I'll look."

I was surprised he hadn't thought to do that already. On the other hand, he wasn't the most astute person I'd ever met.

"Yep, car's still there," he said. "But uhh ... looks like the driver's-side door is open and her bag is on the ground. You know, the one she keeps her clothes in. Her wallet's still sitting here on the counter too."

It was hard for me to believe any woman would leave home without their main lifeline. But I didn't want to worry Tommy more than he already was.

"Let me make a few calls and see if I can find her."

"Okay. Call me back."

I ended the call and tried calling Chief Sheppard again. Still no luck. This time, I had Rose put me through to his machine. I left a message telling him where I was headed, and then I gave him a brief summary of the day's events. Tommy might not have known what happened to Bridget, but I had a feeling I did. I just hoped I'd get to her in time.

# CHAPTER 59

Vicki's car was parked sideways in her driveway, and the trunk was propped open. Dangling from the release handle was a six-inch strand of hair that looked like it had ripped off when it caught in the latch. The trunk's interior was wet, and sitting on the side was a roll of duct tape.

I readied my gun and sprinted toward the front door, which hadn't been closed all the way. I stepped inside. The house was silent except for the heater, which sounded off with a slow hum. I cleared the entryway and front room and moved to the kitchen. An unlit candle rested on the counter next to the refrigerator. I picked it up, instantly recognizing the smell. It was the same aroma I'd caught a whiff of the night I had been knocked unconscious, when I'd mistakenly assumed Charlotte's neighbor had been baking. It hadn't been baked goods at all. The smell had come from a candle—*Vicki's* candle—and must have permeated the clothes she'd been wearing that night.

If only I'd known then that it had been her all along.

The only other item of significance on the counter was a small container of Aconitum napellus, or as Maddie had tagged it, Monkshood, Vicki's drug of choice. I hoped I wasn't too late.

I descended the stairs and turned the corner into the first room. It was empty. I checked the bathroom. Also empty. I neared the second bedroom door and heard someone talking.

"Not a sound, you hear me!" Vicki shouted.

I held my gun in front of me and reached for the door handle. It was locked. I turned to the side aligning myself with the area beneath the knob and kicked—hard. The door banged open.

On a chair in the middle of the room, I spotted Bridget. Her wrists were bound to the chair with rope. From all the years I'd spent with a father who raised me not to be so "girlie," one glance showed me Vicki's skills in the knot-tying department left a lot to be desired. A piece of duct tape had been slapped across Bridget's mouth, and her cheeks were stained with tears. Vicki was positioned behind her, holding a knife to her throat.

"Not what you planned," I said.

She grabbed a mass of Bridget's hair and tightened her grip on the knife.

"Stay where you are," she said. "Don't come any closer."

"The knife doesn't suit you," I said.

She jerked her head to the side. "You think you know so much, don't you?"

"Fake an appraisal, screw a potential client into thinking they scored a great deal on a renovated home, and then you pocket a bunch of extra cash. Sound about right?"

The look on her face said it all.

"And what about Parker Stanton?" I asked. "Where did he come into play in all of this?"

"What does one have to do with another?"

"Since you killed him, I'd say it has everything to do with it. What doesn't make sense to me is—why kill one with poison and the other with a gun?"

"I didn't kill Parker, ever think of that?"

I had.

"Even if you didn't kill Parker, you killed Charlotte and threatened to kill Travis and his family. And now ... well ... everything is falling apart, isn't it?"

"Everything is fine."

I reached into my pocket and pulled out the container of poison I'd found in the kitchen. "Really? I don't think so. And I won't allow you to hurt anyone else."

She gave me a look that said *yeah, right*.

"You won't shoot me," she said. "I bet you don't even know how to use that thing."

I popped off a warning shot about three inches from the side of her head. It settled into the wall behind her. Then I redirected the gun toward her forehead.

"Drop the knife, kick it over to me, and step away from Bridget," I said.

"I'm the one calling the shots here. If you don't want me to slit her throat, you'll toss that gun over to me."

"Not going to happen," I said. "I spoke to the chief of police on my way here. In about a minute, cops will be all over this place."

It was a white lie, but one I hoped would save Bridget's life. Vicki didn't look convinced.

"You're bluffing."

"Let her go, Vicki. It doesn't have to end like this."

She glared at me. "Charlotte. Little Miss Goody Two-shoes. She had everyone wrapped around her real-estate finger. I showed *her*. She wasn't the only one who could make money."

"Except she made it the honest way. You didn't."

"Who cares how I earned it? I'm the one who's still alive."

"You had to kill your partner to get where you are, and for what?"

"Charlotte was leaving me, going to another agency. She said it was time she branched out on her own. After all I did for her, she didn't even care."

"Charlotte wasn't going to another agency," I said. "She was branching out on her own by leaving the country. All she wanted was to help others have a better life. You and your greed stripped it from her."

Vicki stared at me in disbelief. "No, it's not true. Jack said if I didn't do something, she would leave and …"

"And what? He told you to kill her?"

She giggled like a hyena. "What? No. Jack didn't have a clue what was going on. He's far too stupid. His only concern was making sure Charlotte wasn't picked up by another agency. Did you know she planned to rat me out to the board when she finally figured out what I'd been doing?"

"And you decided to stop her before that happened."

"I made a name for myself here. I would have lost my license, and when word spread, I'd be ruined in this town. Getting rid of Charlotte was my only option."

"What happened on the day she died?" I asked.

"I knew she liked to mingle with the guests and have a small glass of wine before heading for her ski run. She was too busy chatting with everyone else to notice me come in. I was in a wig, of course. And when she got up to use the restroom, I did what I needed to do and then stood and watched her finish her drink. It was too easy."

While Vicki continued her rant, Bridget had slowly wiggled out of one of her wrist restraints. I hoped she wouldn't make a move, but as soon as she'd freed herself, she threw a hand up, trying to wrestle the knife out of Vicki's hands. In her attempt to secure it, she stood in front of Vicki, preventing me from getting a clear shot. Vicki lunged at Bridget, slashing her in the side. Bridget fell to the floor.

A gunshot went off, and Vicki collapsed.

She had been hit once in the chest, but I hadn't fired.

I felt a firm grip on my shoulder and swung around, staring into the face of the last person I expected to see.

"You okay?" Coop asked.

I was in shock, so I just stood there, unable to respond. Coop radioed for an ambulance.

Bridget's eyes were closed, and she wasn't moving. I dropped to my knees and pressed my hands over her wound, applying pressure.

Coop bent down next to me.

"Is she going to be all right?" I asked. "There's so much blood."

He assessed the wound. "Yeah, she should be fine. Keep pressure on it just like you're doing."

He pressed two fingers onto Vicki's neck, but there was no need. She was dead.

The ambulance arrived and loaded Bridget inside. She'd lost a lot of blood, but she was going to be all right. I called Tommy and gave him the news, and Coop called the chief and did the same. When he finished, he walked over to me.

"Nick called me when he landed," he said. "He told me you weren't answering your phone, and there was a good chance Vicki had taken Bridget, and I'd find you here, most likely in a heap of trouble."

"I guess I owe you one," I said.

"And I guess you were right about everything."

A compliment from the king of sarcasm. I couldn't believe it.

"Wow, Coop," I said. "Did you really just say I did something right?"

"It doesn't change anything between us."

I patted him on the back and smiled. "No, of course not."

## CHAPTER 60

I sat in the cabana in front of a pool in Las Vegas with an Agatha Christie novel in one hand and a cocktail in the other. It was a cool sixty-seven degrees outside, but I didn't mind. I pulled the blanket I'd brought over my legs and soaked up every second.

"Life is good," Maddie said. "Isn't it?"

I nodded. "And this martini is great."

"You said it. Makes me wonder why we waited so long to come here."

"One of us had a murder to solve. I have to admit, I was shocked to hear from Daniela after everything was all over. I couldn't believe it when I checked my mailbox at the office and she'd paid for an all-inclusive trip for this weekend to thank me for rescuing her."

Maddie stood. "Well, be sure to thank her again from me. This is fabulous. The pool is calling my name. What do you think? You up for a swim?"

I shook my head. "Way too cold for me to even consider it, but I might get in the hot tub later."

She grabbed her towel off the chair. "Fine, wuss."

Charlotte's murder had been solved, and I took a great deal of satisfaction in knowing Audrey finally had the truth she deserved.

Parker's unusual suicide still bothered me, but I'd resigned myself to the fact that I hadn't been hired to look into his murder. Whatever had or hadn't happened, it wasn't my responsibility.

I dog-eared a page in *Murder on the Orient Express* and adjusted my chair. I had just started to drift off when my cell phone rang. The screen identified the call as unknown. I sent it to voicemail and relaxed back into my chair. A minute later, it rang again. I sent it to voicemail once more. When it rang a third time, I was annoyed enough to pick it up.

"Good afternoon," a man said.

The voice was unfamiliar.

"Who is this?" I asked.

"Look to your right."

I glanced over my shoulder and saw a man dressed in a suit sitting at a table about ten yards from me. He was surrounded by an entourage of men who looked like bouncers at a Las Vegas nightclub. The man made a gesture with two of his fingers, and the entourage stood in unison and went their separate ways.

One member of the entourage headed in my direction, tipped his head at me, and winked as he passed. I gasped, recognizing him as the man in black. For a moment, time stood still, and I forgot all about the cell phone still resting on my ear.

"I would like a moment of your time," the man said.

He waved me over and ended the call.

I looked for Maddie, who had been joined in the pool by a man eager for her attention. I was reluctant to walk over to meet the mysterious man who'd just called me, but we were outside in the middle of the day in public, and if Maddie ever looked up, she could see where I'd gone. I wrapped a towel around my waist and walked over. He pulled a chair out for me and invited me to sit down. I did.

The man had short, black hair, tanned skin, and looked to be in his late thirties. He reminded me of a young Cary Grant.

Everything about him, from the expensive watch on his wrist to his tailored suit, told me he was refined and sophisticated.

"Who are you?" I asked.

"There's no need to be alarmed," he said. "My name is Giovanni Luciana."

Of course it was.

He offered me his hand. I took it. He placed his other hand over mine and held it there for a moment. In my awkwardness, I pulled back.

"Any relation to Daniela Luciana?" I asked.

"She is my sister. I believe you offered her a ride home not too long ago, after she found herself in an unfortunate circumstance."

"And now you're following me?"

He crossed one leg over the other. "My family is one of the owners of this hotel."

"Oh, I see."

"I had a vested interest in your case. Congratulations, by the way."

"Did you have a vested interest in Parker Stanton too?" I asked.

"I may have."

"Strange the way he died, don't you think? I'm interested in hearing your thoughts about what happened."

"I'm equally as interested in hearing yours."

"All right. Since you asked, I believe Parker was murdered and whoever killed him made it look like he committed suicide."

He laced his fingers together and rested them on the table. "That's quite an accusation."

"It's not wrong, though, is it?"

"I found his treatment of women unacceptable. Men like Parker Stanton don't deserve the life they have. They think they can do whatever they like because they have money. Men like that need to be dealt with."

"So you what, dealt with it?" I asked.

I sat there a moment, shocked at the bluntness of my words.

He reached inside his jacket pocket, and I felt a sudden urge to run. I was relieved when he pulled out a business card and handed it to me, but surprised to see only one thing was printed on it: a phone number.

"You did my sister a service, and for that I'm grateful to you," he said. "Should you ever need anything from me, call the number on the card."

"Anything like ... what? Aren't you worried I'll go to the police?"

"You could, but I don't think you will."

"Why not?"

"I believe we share some commonalities. We both seek justice and do whatever it takes to get it."

"I understand how it felt when you found out what Parker did to Daniela, but taking another person's life isn't your decision to make."

He rose from his chair, snapped his fingers, and two men from his entourage reappeared.

"You'll have to excuse me," he said. "I have other business to attend to. Perhaps our paths will cross again in the future, and we can resume the conversation."

"What about my questions? You haven't answered them yet."

He started to walk away and then turned back. "I enjoy your passion, Miss Monroe. Don't ever change."

Thank you so much for reading BLACK DIAMOND DEATH!

This is the first book in a lifelong series, and I hope you enjoyed reading book one and the introduction into the world of the feisty, OCD-challenged Sloane Monroe as much as I have enjoyed writing her over the years. There's so much more to come in the series, but first in book two, we dive into the tragic, horrifying death of Sloane's sister Gabrielle, and we follow Sloane as she tracks the serial killer responsible for Gabrielle's murder.

# Praise for Murder in Mind:

*"Bradshaw writes a great thriller, with likeable characters, and a taunt timeline that keeps you reading way past lights-out."* —Robin Landry, Amazon Top 1,000 Reviewer

*"The suspense never lets up. You can't put it down."* Warren A. Lewis, Amazon Top Fiction Contributor

*"The similarities to Stephanie Plum make it a fun read."* Robin Landry, Amazon Top Reviewer

*"One thing is certain: Bradshaw can keep the pages turning."* Michael Robertson, Bestselling Author of The Shadow Order series.

*"The author does a great job of detailing the crimes and gives you just the right amount of "hook" to keep the pages turning."* Christopher Blewitt, Bestselling Author of The Lost Journal

*"Only once in a while do you come upon a novel that sweeps you literally off your feet. The pot-boiling tension in this story is out of this world."* Cheryl Bradshaw can write like the pros did at the turn of the 20th century."* Glen Cantrell, Author of The Resume

# About Cheryl Bradshaw

Cheryl Bradshaw is a *New York Times* and *USA Today* bestselling author writing in the genres of mystery, thriller, paranormal suspense, and romantic suspense. Her novel *Stranger in Town* (Sloane Monroe series #4) was a 2013 Shamus Award finalist for Best PI Novel of the Year, and her novel *I Have a Secret* (Sloane Monroe series #3) was a 2013 eFestival of Words winner for Best Thriller. Since 2013, seven of Cheryl's novels have made the *USA Today* bestselling books list.

# Books by Cheryl Bradshaw

## Sloane Monroe Series

**Black Diamond Death** (Book 1)
*Charlotte Halliwell has a secret. But before revealing it to her sister, she's found dead.*

**Murder in Mind** (Book 2)
*A woman is found murdered, the serial killer's trademark "S" carved into her wrist.*

**I Have a Secret** (Book 3)
*Doug Ward has been running from his past for twenty years. But after his fourth whisky of the night, he doesn't want to keep quiet, not anymore.*

**Stranger in Town** (Book 4)
*A frantic mother runs down the aisles, searching for her missing daughter. But little Olivia is already gone.*

**Bed of Bones** (Book 5)
*Sometimes even the deepest, darkest secrets find their way to the surface.*

**Flirting with Danger** (Book 5.5) A Sloane Monroe Short Story
*A fancy hotel. A weekend getaway. For Sloane Monroe, rest has finally arrived, until the lights go out, a woman screams, and Sloane's nightmare begins.*

**Hush Now Baby** (Book 6)
*Serena Westwood tiptoes to her baby's crib and looks inside, startled to find her newborn son is gone.*

**Dead of Night** (Book 6.5) A Sloane Monroe Short Story
*After her mother-in-law is fatally stabbed, Wren is seen fleeing with the bloody knife. Is Wren the killer, or is a dark, scandalous family secret to blame?*

**Gone Daddy Gone** (Book 7)
*A man lurks behind Shelby in the park. Who is he? And why does he have a gun?*

**Smoke & Mirrors** (Book 8)
Grace Ashby wakes to the sound of a horrifying scream. She races down the hallway, finding her mother's lifeless body on the floor in a pool of blood. Her mother's boyfriend Hugh is hunched over her, but is Hugh really her mother's killer?

Sloane Monroe Stories: Deadly Sins

**Deadly Sins: Sloth** (Book 1)
*Darryl has been shot, and a mysterious woman is sprawled out on the floor in his hallway. She's dead too. Who is she? And why have they both been murdered?*

### Deadly Sins: Wrath (Book 2)
*Headlights flash through Maddie's car's back windshield, someone following close behind. When her car careens into a nearby tree, the chase comes to an end. But for Maddie, the end is just the beginning.*

### Deadly Sins: Lust (Book 3)
*Marissa Calhoun sits alone on a beach-like swimming hole nestled on Australia's foreshore. Tonight the lagoon is hers and hers alone. Or is it?*

## Addison Lockhart Series

### Grayson Manor Haunting (Book 1)
*When Addison Lockhart inherits Grayson Manor after her mother's untimely death, she unlocks a secret that's been kept hidden for over fifty years.*

### Rosecliff Manor Haunting (Book 2)
*Addison Lockhart jolts awake. The dream had seemed so real. Eleven-year-old twins Vivian and Grace were so full of life, but they couldn't be. They've been dead for over forty years.*

### Blackthorn Manor Haunting (Book 3)
*Addison Lockhart leans over the manor's window, gasping when she feels a hand on her back. She grabs the windowsill to brace herself, but it's too late—she's already falling.*

Belle Manor Haunting (Book 4) Coming Winter 2019

# Till Death do us Part Novella Series

### Whispers of Murder (Book 1)
*It was Isabelle Donnelly's wedding day, a moment in time that should have been the happiest in her life...until it ended in murder.*

### Echoes of Murder (Book 2)
*When two women are found dead at the same wedding, medical examiner Reagan Davenport will stop at nothing to discover the identity of the killer.*

## Stand-Alone Novels

### Eye for Revenge
*Quinn Montgomery wakes to find herself in the hospital. Her childhood best friend Evie is dead, and Evie's four-year-old son witnessed it all. Traumatized over what he saw, he hasn't spoken.*

### The Perfect Lie
*When true-crime writer Alexandria Weston is found murdered on the last stop of her book tour, fellow writer Joss Jax steps in to investigate.*

### Hickory Dickory Dead
*Maisie Fezziwig wakes to a harrowing scream outside. Curious, she walks outside to investigate, and Maisie stumbles on a grisly murder that will change her life forever.*

### Roadkill
*Suburban housewife Juliette Granger has been living a secret life ... a life that's about to turn deadly for everyone she loves.*

## Non-Fiction

### Arise

*Arise is a collection of motivational stories written by women who have been where you may find yourself today. Their stories are raw, real, heartfelt, and inspiring.*

Printed in Great Britain
by Amazon